SCARCITY

DAVID J WINTERS

{Subgenre:Publishers}

CONTENTS

Also by David J. Winters v

Prologue 1
Prologue 9
1. Garden Party 19
2. Survivor Bias 23
3. Eminence Grise 26
4. Down on the Farm 29
5. Tater 35
6. Minimal Lethal 38
7. Not Gonna Lie... 44
8. Vanishing Act 46
9. Invocation 51
10. Emergency Management 54
11. Tarred and I Wanna go to Bed 57
12. Necessity is the Mother... 60
13. Klaatu Barada Nikto 63
14. Intentions 67
15. At Home 73
16. Flipping Switches 83
17. Limitless Abundance 86
18. Rats in the Manger 89
19. Think it Over 92
20. Food, Nest, Water 97
21. Normal 100
Epilogue 104

ALSO BY DAVID J. WINTERS

BEDSIDE MANNER

Nurse-and-union-leader *turned* homicide-detective, Eminence Gray, uses her gifts of empathy and emotional labor to catch the most vicious of West Brandon's killers. Em's ability to maintain this skillset will be put to the ultimate test when the highest-profile murder case her department has ever faced falls right into her lap. Add to Em's troubles a corrupt executive from her union days, back and up to old tricks, and it might just be Eminence Gray requiring a little *bedside manner*... or a lot.

INTERVENTIONISM

Roger Jech doesn't have any superpowers, but he has a super ability: harm him, harm yourself in equal measure. Hit him with a right hook, your jaw breaks. Shoot him in the head, your brains blow out the back of you. Drop him in a war zone, your enemies kill themselves killing him. Jech's a weapon to the wrong people and a saviour to the right, but before he can become the former, he must learn to harness his gift before it becomes his curse.

THE TAKING OF SHALE CITY

Shale City has seen better days. First, the dam burst, flooding out the town's iron mine. Then, local officials shut down the shipping and courier services, the only thing keeping Shale City hanging on... It was all the mayor of Shale could do to fight off the more 'legitimate' of sleazeballs trying to destroy her city, but now it seems as though some other kind of sleazeball force is encroaching upon her town, set on putting the final nail in its coffin...

Scarcity
Copyright © 2024 by David J. Winters
All rights reserved.

No part of this book may be reproduced in any form or by any electronic or mechanical means, including information storage and retrieval systems, without written permission from the author, except for the use of brief quotations in a book review.

This is a work of fiction. All of the characters, organizations, and events portrayed in this novel are in the future and the future hasn't happened yet.

ISBN 9781068863639 (paperback) | ISBN 9781068863622 (hardcover) | ISBN 9781068863615 (electronic book)

{SubGenre : Publishers}
www.subgenrepublishers.com

For Dad and Waylon Jennings

To the former for introducing me to the music of the latter and to the latter for the music that played while I wrote

Waylon! Waylon! Waylon!

PROLOGUE
A PROBLEM

It was just your average nondescript urban setting back then. A lot of concrete, steel, glass... Blocky and tallish ranging to not-so-tallish in all its conglomeration. Conglomeration is architectural.

Did I mention that this architecture rests gently on a bed of even more concrete? Well, it does.

There you are.

Now go ahead, close your eyes and try to picture what was just described. Nothing much specific comes to mind does it? Told you it was *nondescript*.

Let's add a little uniqueness...

Back then the city faced a crisis... of sorts. A mild crisis, but a crisis nonetheless. Rats!

What's so unique about a city with a rat problem?

What if I told you there were lots and lots of rats? Still not impressed? I forget sometimes, your world has yet to solve so many of the quotidian concerns my world solved long ago. Now, I don't mean to sound supercilious or anything of the sort. I just forget sometimes where everyone's at in terms of development and progression.

As I intend to explain, this progress is really just a quirk of instinct. It rests in all of us social creatures, activated when its activated. My peoples' was activated first is all, where I have every faith that we'll all get there soon enough.

That said, the rat problem would certainly be anomalous by my world's standards, just maybe not yours... yet. It's really not the *problem* that made the situation so interesting anyway, but the *solution*.

Let's take a closer look at the city...

How about we take a look at the city's financial district, street level?

Despite the wealth and prosperity evident, our concerning number of rats move about the street and sidewalks with seeming impunity. Pedestrians dodge and weave, and stumble on designer heels and slip on designer soles, all in an effort to avoid contact.

The rats are not afraid.

IN AN EFFORT TO SOLVE the problem, the mayor's office put out bounties on the rodents.

A bored-looking office *Drone* sits at the reception desk of the centralized location of one of the city's many bureaucracies. A sign over her left shoulder reads,

 1 Rat = .0001% tax rebate (compounded)

A man, grinning in anticipated satisfaction, holding a milk crate in front of a shirt with some conspicuous red splotches on it, approaches Drone's desk. Soon as he gets to it he turns his milk crate upside down sending several dozen bloodied rat corpses tumbling out and rolling across the desk's surface.

The bounty program failed...

The Drone recoils instantly, backing herself up against the wall behind her. She flops her hands up and down and hops in disgust. She hops in not just disgust but also despair. The source of her despair are the men and women, all with milk crates in hands, in a lineup starting at her desk and stretching out the office door and on for blocks.

IN RESPONSE TO THE FAILED bounty program, the city *of course* kept it but amended the conditions for collecting.

The same bored-looking Drone sits at her reception station. She's since calmed, calmed right back into the kind of boredom she's come to depend on being the face of the *Bureau of Affairs Made Excessively Convoluted*...

That's not really the name, but you all know of bureaucracies too well - being of your time and place. Of what happens when anyone attempts to control a vastly complex system from the top down, as though by puppet master. That is,

Anyone sufficiently capable of fulfilling the role of puppet master is smart enough to know to never attempt it and doesn't.

Of course, the inverse also applies, that is,

Anyone dumb enough to think it possible to fulfill such a role, is too dumb to fulfill it but will drag everyone down trying.

But you all know this.

Or, maybe you don't. If I recall, my people often failed to notice these beasts of convolution. The effects of their growing number of hapless constituents were so slowly and insidiously imposed that by the time we *did* notice - if we noticed them at all - it became shockingly apparent that because of them, the mighty oak that used to be our society was now more termite than tree.

Often, the few of us made aware became *so* after having ventured off - but not before much red tape – to some other land without the same gross inefficiencies as ours. That land's gross *Efficiency* promptly slapped us in the face by virtue of contrast.

Was it any better to be in the know? Arguably, not. Once we were made aware of our inordinately large termite-to-tree ratio, the realization that immediately followed was this, despite the problem of termites slowly killing our - and *indifferently* their - home in their feeding, we couldn't simply remove them as they had made themselves the primary source of structure. The 'tree' would simply collapse into its own hollowness free of those bugs of officiousness padding it out. What could a society do?

More on that later...

The altered sign on the wall behind The Drone now reads:

1 Rat TAIL = .0001% tax rebate (compounded). Tails only!

We're in the basement of a home of another man grinning in anticipated satisfaction. He's tending to a huge number of cages. The cages contain rats. The *Rat Tender* is feeding the large quantity of rats a larger quantity of food pellets.

He finishes dispensing the feed and picks up a pair of garden sheers. With his free work-gloved hand, he lifts one of the rats out of its cage. Grinning wider, the Tender inches his sheers towards the rat's tail. Sheer blades are just about to snip when...

SEVERAL DOZEN RAT TAILS PLOP down onto Drone's desk. Rat Tender's still got that grin. Drone frowns. She's not *as* disgusted with the results of this compromise, but she sure isn't happy about it.

BACK IN THE FINANCIAL DISTRICT, hundreds of rats scurry in waves up the sidewalk, *sans tails.*

The amended bounty program failed too.

All iterations of the bounty program were suspended immediately.

All Rat Tenders released any remaining caged rats immediately. All thousands and thousands of them...

. . .

THANKS TO THE CITY'S EFFORTS, there were more rats than ever. No matter what they had tried, they couldn't lick the problem. Every measure seemed to have only worsened things. The problem looked like it was never going to go away, until, one day...

It did.

THE STREETS OF THE FINANCIAL district are now free of pests. Almost. There're still yuppies... but no rats. Otherwise, it's pristine sidewalks and streets. Uncanny.

How? It certainly wasn't the city's doing. Although they, without any hesitation, took sole credit for the outcome.

The mayor, an all-purpose suit, speaks animatedly and imploringly to the people and the press. He speaks from the steps of Town Hall. He talks of how the city implemented the bounty program and, shortly after, the problem was resolved. *What else could have done it but the bounties?* he suggests.

He was employing that impeccably boneheaded etiological logic,

Something good happened, we did something before that, therefore what we did before made that something good happen.

The press buy it wholesale, the people do not.

The people knew about the rat farms. Hell, most of them did the farming. They knew about the failure of the initiative as, the second the initiative ended, they could still see their inventory. The rats didn't simply vanish into thin air. Though their worth was made to vanish by stroke of pen. The inventory just kept staring those Rat Tenders in their faces with tiny little faces all their own.

Offer to buy a man's despair for its weight in gold and watch how fast his stock dwindles to hope. In this case, hope in a profitable tomorrow. A cruel trick as despair yields *prize* and *prize* yields hope and hope negates despair. Prize is forfeit, hastening despair's renewal. The cycle begins again. So it goes until the shop is closed. A cruel trick. Worse, despair the losing of the game too and you end up with more unmovable stock than when you started.

The people knew how much of the problem remained because the embodiment of their despair scurried ceaselessly and limitlessly at their feet. Scurried ceaselessly and limitlessly at *everyone's* feet for weeks after the halting of that program.

The people knew and the mayor had broken the golden rule of governance (excerpt from Macky O'Malley's *The Idiot Prince*):

> To maintain the appearance of competency and effectiveness, never attempt any initiative that may actually bring about a beneficial outcome. Never attempt any initiative that may bring about *any* outcome. Simply assess your current state of affairs, identify a beneficial outcome on its way due to a world of causes outside of your doing, then announce that you've earmarked several million dollars toward the end of achieving this already inevitable outcome. Earmark billions if the economy you're leeching off is large enough.
>
> When the outcome results, claim the initiative you funded caused it. At this point, I must remind, *do not* under any circumstances fund any actual initiative. As well, make sure you spend the earmarked funds so no one discovers them in your coffers and wonders how money necessary to bring about a beneficial outcome wasn't actually spent in bringing it about. Take a nice vacation or something...

Now for the flip side of this principle.

When bad things are happening that won't just fix themselves, whether or not you the elected official are the cause - where, let's face it, you are - pass the buck.

Call the first part of this principle, *The Sunrise Dictum*. Call it this because the recommended course of action is akin to shouting *rise* at the dawn horizon and taking credit for the sun coming up. It's an age-old technique employed by political actors everywhere intended to excuse their only ever engaging in empty posturing, their changing of nothing, and their taking of credit for beneficial outcomes despite only ever engaging in empty posturing and the changing of nothing.

For whatever reason, the principle fools enough people enough of the time. Just make sure, if you ever intend on employing it, that whatever feckless initiative you've proposed doesn't end before the problem gets worse, because...

There's a hint of growing agitation apparent in the mayor. He's becoming more animated. He doesn't appear to be winning anyone over.

Maybe if he flails some more?

PROLOGUE
A SOLUTION

City Hall didn't solve the problem. Not the mayor nor anyone on council. Nor did the problem simply resolve itself. It was a local inventor and experimenter who licked it. A man with nothing but ingenuity, a knack for scavenging, and a hypothesis on his hands.

THE INVENTOR EXITS HIS SMALL coupe in front of his two-bedroom bungalow. The bungalow is the same degree of *small for a house* as the coupe is *small for a car*. *Cozy*, is the better word. Nicer too. He picks up a cloth-covered square object from across the driver's seat, and carries it toward his front door.

He carries it into the house and all the way down the basement steps. Steps are lit, hardly at all, by a forty watt lightbulb. They lead into darkness otherwise. At the bottom of the steps The Inventor reaches for a switch that will illuminate the lab where he is to test his hypothesis. His hypothesis is thus,

Given a large enough number of discrete populations...

FLIP! Light floods the basement lab revealing a bare floor with row upon row of rectangular boxes. The boxes have glass tops and wooden sides as well as a crosswise chunk at their centers. The chunk acts as a divider, separating the box into two opposing chambers. Any given chunk has three plastic intake tubes protruding out its top.

Of any particular sentient being...

The inventor whips the cloth cover off the box he's carrying. *Even. More. Rats.* He pulls out two of the rodents and drops one each into the opposing chambers of one of the boxes. Inside each chamber we see a single paddle and three dispensers of some sort. Both rats sniff at their respective paddles, curious.

Evolving over a long enough period of time...

We see that there are many pairs of opposing rats in many of those boxes. Some are just sniffing at their paddles, like the most recent tenants. A few are curled up, looking around but otherwise ignoring the paddles altogether. A few others however, are depressing the paddles according to no particular pattern.

The inventor removes a pair of lethargic rats and replaces them with two more new recruits.

SOME TIME HAS PASSED. MOST rats sleep in their pens. Curiously, one pair is still tapping away at their respective paddles. You'd almost swear they were doing so in a semi-deliberate manner. Inventor continues swapping out the lethargic rats with more energetic ones.

A functional society will emerge...

It seems the pair still tapping have figured something out. The first-chamber rat, call him *Fat*, taps his paddle as a sip of water is dispensed on the second-chamber rat's side. Call the second-chamber rat *Sat*. Sat drinks-up, then immediately depresses her paddle sending a similar sized sip, in reciprocity, to Fat. Turns out the function of either paddle is to cycle through the distribution of a piece of food, a piece of material for nest building, and a drink of water. One tap *food*, one tap *nesting*, one tap *water*, then back to food on the fourth tap. These resources always go to the rat in the opposing chamber. It's as simple as that.

If we were to look down on Sat and Fat from a bird's eye view we'd see the rats engaged in a *you-give/I-give* relationship of tap tap tapping. However, if we were to look in on just, say, Fat's chamber and linger a second, we'd get the impression that the causality of the interactions is so much simpler. Because either rat is completely unaware its neighbor is providing all of the resources, for all they can observe, the function of the paddle works according to two basic rules,

1. Don't have a resource and want one? Hit the paddle and the machine rewards you.
2. Rewarded by the machine without hitting the paddle? Better hit the paddle quick, almost like a thank you, or it might stop rewarding you in the future.

The center chunk dividing the pair denies them any sense of the cooperation necessary for their survival.

Hierarchies and all...

Fat receives a ball of yarn from his materials dispenser. He attempts to pull it from the dispenser but a strand is hung up inside the mechanism. He pulls and pulls, finally breaking it free. He runs the yarn to his nest then turns back for the paddle as though desperately trying to *not* break with routine.

Fat's about to press the paddle but stops. Something's off. A sound can be heard. It's a tapping coming from the other side of the chamber. Sat must have gotten impatient not receiving her materials. She's making a second attempt.

A bonus food pellet shoots out at Fat.

You'd almost swear Fat's just experienced an epiphany. He waits some more and the tapping begins anew...

FAT AND SAT ARE STILL working like a well-oiled machine, tapping away. Only, Fat is just tapping every three dispenses, racking up three times the amount of resources as Sat.

Driven by nothing but the instinct to satisfy ones appetites.

The pair is just going *tap tap tap*; *eat eat eat*; *drink drink drink*; *nest nest nest*; *tap tap tap*... non-stop, at maximal efficiency. Fat benefits disproportionally, but both have an unending supply of essential resources.

YOU COULD SAY THE INVENTOR got the evidence he was looking for, but you'd likely also want to ask, how did any of this solve the problem of the city's rat infestation?

By accident of compassion.

NEXT TO THE ROWS OF rat chambers in The Inventor's lab sits a large pen, covering roughly the same area as the collection of chambers reserved for the paddle-pushers. Turns out the pen is reserved for the rats that never learned the pattern.

The Inventor picks up an under-fed and under-watered rat from one of the rectangular boxes and moves him to the big pen. The pen is open concept, no inner walls, just paddle pedestals lining the inside perimeter. There are rats already in the pen, fully rejuvenated, flipping those paddles, eating, drinking, and maintaining nests. These paddles require no reciprocity, it's just one push one unit of whichever resource was next in the cycle. There are way more paddles than there are rats.

Inventor places the exhausted rat at a paddle and hangs a food pellet above its head. The exhausted creature lifts itself up to reach the food, inadvertently using the paddle to gain some leverage. This releases an alternative food pellet. He tries reaching again, releasing some nesting... then reaches again, releasing water... then again and again... more food... more housing... more water... then... he forgets about the dangling food pellet altogether. He's stuffed.

Understand, a less compassionate person could have just let the unlucky rats starve to death. The Inventor could have saved a lot of effort and resources feeding the dead rats to the live ones. Disgusting, I know, but don't worry....

Inventor pours 'Ol Roy dog food into the hopper from which the food pellets - dog food evidently - are dispensed. He had planned for the contingency that most rats would not figure out the pattern. He made sure they were well-accommodated. Perhaps *too* well-accommodated. The saving of these rats turned out to yield better experimental data than the paddle-pushing rats ever could.

AT FIRST, THE RATS IN the open-concept pen are just *tap tap tapping* away at their pedestals, non-stop. Their nests are massive, full of excess housing and food hoarded on instinct. Then, something curious happens.

The Inventor lays another spent rat in front of a paddle and begins tying the food pellet in place. Before he can finish, another rat approaches. The visiting rat gets up on his hind legs. He squeaks in the other rat's direction, then turns, squeaking towards the pedestal. He gets on all fours again and walks over to the pedestal.

Tap tap tap.

The visitor dispenses a unit of food, housing, and water for the exhausted rat. He then turns, and just walks away.

The Inventor looks intrigued.

The spent rat lumbers and reaches for what looks like the food at first, but then lumbers right past and hits the paddle. He's learned.

All the open-concept rats are learning. What will they discover next?

Lesson Number One: Hoarding is futile when resources are easily accessible and inexhaustible.

The Inventor soon noticed that the various resources he provided only needed replenishing a fraction of the time.

The paddles are near always deserted. Completely inactive. The rats are happy with what they need.

Lesson Number Two: There's such a thing as leisure.

A rat rolls a food pellet around, seemingly disinterested. She walks away from it and curls up in her nest, looks bored.

Lesson Number Three: Leisure isn't worth a damn if you don't maximize the quality of it.

Some rats play fight.
Some rats sleep.
Some rats have intercourse.
More rats sleep.
More rats have intercourse.
More rats sleep.
Other rats sleep.
Other other rats sleep.

Lesson Number Four: If everything you know bores you, know more.

A more ingenious rat has managed to break out of the pen. She scurries, without hesitation, up the wall and into an open piece of ductwork. Open, save for some fiberglass insulation keeping the air in. The rat pulls it out with ease.

Explorer Rat pushes open, and emerges from, a vent cover in the kitchen.

The Inventor's house *Cleaner* is in the dining room area. She's standing on a step-stool cleaning the fan over the dinner table. She's mechanical about it, swooshing one of those flat fluff dusters across a fan blade. She swooshes across one blade then rotates the fan to clean the next. She's swooshing and rotating, swooshing and rotating, when... She stops abruptly. Her eyes widen. She's frozen.

Explorer Rat is clinging to the top of the fan blade. She's looking at the cleaner with curiosity. She gets up on her hind legs and sniffs in Cleaner's direction. Then...

*Squeak.

Cleaner breaks from her trance, erupting in screams. She starts swinging the duster at the rat, back and forth, back and forth. She connects on the third pass and sends Explorer flying into a laundry basket full of dish towels, dish rags, and pot holders. At the very moment Cleaner connects, she loses her balance and starts windmilling her arms, only delaying the inevitable. She tumbles backwards, then downwards, then out of sight.

THE INVENTOR IS TRYING TO console an irate cleaning lady. She's shaking her left fist and holding her aching head in her right hand. Her lips are moving rapidly... angrily too.

THE INVENTOR FINISHES REINFORCING THE rat pen. Upon completion, he frustratedly throws his needle-nosed pliers into the corner, then storms off. The Explorer Rat as well as others observe this with what almost looks like concern.

Final Lesson: If you're attempting to brave the unknown, don't hassle the locals.

The Cleaner is back, doing what she does... must have gotten a raise. She's in the kitchen again, moving various appliances and wiping under, behind, and around them. It seems mundane at first, but...

We move in on an oven mitt that she's just set to one side. As she moves away from it, Explorer Rat's head pokes out from the opening. The rat looks in Cleaner's direction while Cleaner looks away but, the second Cleaner initiates the turning of her head to look back, Explorer recedes into the mitt and out of sight. The Cleaner doesn't have a clue...

...But the Inventor does. He watches the scene from the kitchen doorway, staying out of sight at all the right instances himself.

Again, he's intrigued.

THAT WAS THE SOLUTION. NOT trying to get rid of the rats but, instead, harnessing an instinct they always had in them.

A rat scurries down a gutter. The rodent's acting in a calculated manner, staying invisible to the people occupying the heavily populated street. There are many many rats out and about in the city streets as a matter of fact, but only where free from the eyes of the people.

The rat bolts out of the gutter and scurries up the downspout of an eavestrough. He peeks out of a tear in the side of the spout about two-thirds up. Coast is clear. He leaps from the tear and disappears into a hole in the wall left by a missing brick.

The instinct the rats harnessed was one of unobtrusive coexistence, only expressible on a single condition, *limitless abundance.*

Inside the wall of the building, on the other side of that missing brick, we hear a *tap tap tapping.* Imagine the wall's gone. Imagine it's like we're looking at a bisection of this side of the building. What we'd see in the small space between the floorboards of the floor above and the ceiling of the floor below is an abundance of dispenser pedestals, their resources inexhaustible to all rats of the city who may ever desire to occupy them. *Tap, tap, tap, tap, tap...*

Moving up the bisected building, we see in each space between floors the same setup, rat homes and resource dispensers.

We're picking up speed as we climb. We see that it's floor after floor of dispensers. We confirm this feature at each floor as we rocket up past the penthouse of the impossibly tall skyscraper and on into the sky!

WELL, THAT TOOK CARE OF the rats. What about the rest of us?

1

GARDEN PARTY

It's a forest in the northwest. Oaks, maples, poplars. We move through it. It's dark but we can make out much of the setting by moonlight. We're through the bush and into a clearing, pushing in on a chain-link-surrounded compound. Fence looks to only serve to keep non-human animals out. Ivy grows all across it and two thirds up. Lush green by physics but grey to the eye under dark of night.

Moving through the fence we see the ivy isn't as thick as it first appeared. It's just superimposed with what's inside the compound, a vast array of horticulture stretching for miles in only an eighth-of-a-square-mile of space. The only thing interrupting the fruitful vastness is an agrarian longhouse a couple hundred yards from the gate. Scene's totally surreal otherwise.

We stop on a potato patch. Looks like a dragon's back in that moonlight. Back starts breaking out in boils... Four men, armed, goggled, and in camouflage rise as they canter in lock-step toward the longhouse.

At the end of the patch they halt, assuming a crouching formation. Whatever they're doing is all rote so far, so, *so far so good*. The leader of the team, codename *Nike 1*, commands with chopping ostensive gestures. *Go! Go!* Another of the team, codename *Nike 3*, begins a reconnoiter. He's off to skulk along the longhouse periphery to see what he can see...

After a bit of a beat, he returns.

"Breach point?" whispers Nike 1.

"Negative. No entry," Nike 3 answers in similar whisper.

"How?"

"No doors."

"You're kidding... They weren't born in there."

"No *goddamn* doors," Nike 3 insists.

"Contingencies? Nike 2?"

Nike 2 taps a finger to his right ear. "Nike 2 to Kool-Aid. Intel's for crap. Repeat, intel's for crap. Need entry solution for wall-banger."

The teams' headsets come alive with the voice of their operations officer, codename *Kool-Aid*. "Negative. Door knocker's still a go," crackles the disembodied voice.

"Get over yourself," Nike 2 chides. "No door to knock on. Intel's no good."

"I'm looking at three points of entry," Kool-Aid insists.

"Put down your farmer's almanac, Kool-Aid. Here in *the world* all we can see is-"

"Drone has eyes on the structure," Kool-Aid interrupts.

THE ROOM'S BUZZING WITH TECH and about a half dozen people operating it. A large video monitor shows a thermal imaging of the compound. On monitor in mid-ground we see the ops team as a semi-amorphous four-headed blob of heat. Team's red at the center, fading outward into orange, further to yellow at the periphery. In background, we see the longhouse. Additional blobs of heat are lining the left half of the house. Occupants appear to be in bunk beds, stacked two-by-two.

Kool-Aid stands at the center of the room, staring at the monitor screen, talking into a head-set. He's continuing his conversation with Nike 2.

"You're wearing that non-regulation boonie you think makes you look like Billy from *Predator*..."

On monitor, Nike 2's head twists backwards near owl-like trying to catch the distant drone.

"Looking around now..." Kool-Aid narrates. "Still looking..."

Nike 2 catches sight of it.

"Now you got us, Nike 2."

On the monitor, doors are clearly visible on the longhouse. Thermal people are still inside too.

BACK IN THE COMPOUND...

THEY'RE not. None of the team see anything through their night vision viewfinders. Doors visible on the ops center monitors are gone. Maybe there are inhabitants behind those walls, maybe not.

Then...

BOOM! A door materializes on the longhouse. *BOOM!* A second door. *BOOM!* Third door. *BOOM!* Fourth door. And, finally, *BOOM!* Fifth door.

All of the ops team are reacting to this surreality so it's no hallucination. Nike 2 takes off his goggles, still looking in disbelief.

"There's too many..."

Another *BOOM!*

A sourceless light engulfs the team. All members bolt upright, silent, still, like they've been told to freeze though nobody's told them to do anything.

They stand rigid, bathed in white light.

OPS CENTER MONITOR IS SOLID red. Burning hot. Impossible.

Kool-Aid stares at it silently. Then...

SWOOSH!

Screen goes completely greyscale. Zero thermal energy. Impossible.

Everyone in the room is exercised by this, everyone but Kool-Aid. Some of the techs move about going from terminal to terminal. Some rapidly tap at keyboards. Some flip switches. Kool-Aid just peers at the screen cooly, pensive.

His eyes narrow.

2

SURVIVOR BIAS

CSIS Headquarters*. Ottawa, Amerika East.

It's your standard sterile boardroom. There's a large elliptical table with agents of various investigative and intelligence organizations of Amerika East seated around it. About a couple dozen men and women of all shapes and sizes save for one odd universal, they're old. *Special Agent Dana Lorre* is the only person in the room standing. She's running the show. Show's almost over.

"Before we break, I'd like to reiterate, this interagency stuff is never easy at the best of times. Your cooperation on such short notice is greatly appreciated."

There's some nodding, looks of facile approval, that silent clapping of hands that ends just before palms connect. Clapping's directed arbitrarily at various attendees by other attendees. They nod at each other as they do this like they're not sure if the nodding means *no, really, you deserve this, thank you* or *thank you, I deserve this, no really.*

"Alright, we reconvene this afternoon," Lorre says. She points at an ATF agent and a Mountie. "ATF and RCMP will brief us on the

---

* *CSIS* is pronounced *see-sis* (like *see-saw*, but stupider).

agrarians and any new militia activity." She points at two FBI agents. "And FBI will give us what they got on..." She stifles a little. "T-the numbers... *Numbers*! Jesus. Just tell us guys, they at least take fewer of us this week than last?"

Bureau agents just shake their heads. News is always worse than yesterday's and yet Lorre always reacts as though a hope's been dashed...

"We reconvene this afternoon."

MEETING ATTENDEES BEGIN TO DISPERSE. They don't appear to be in any rush. As they clear away we see *Agent Bart* sitting comfortably on a couch along the wall of the boardroom. Lorre catches sight of him and he rises to greet her.

"Surprise, surprise, they leave all the bureaucrats," he jokes, trying to break a little of tension's neck.

Lorre smiles in good humor. "Horse's ass ya. Survivor bias."

"How so?"

"Twenty-ones to forty-fives are gone and if you're older than that around here all you're good for is bureaucracy."

"Let's test that," Bart says a little wry. "I want on this."

Lorre looks heartened at this but suppresses any eagerness otherwise.

"A team? How? Just us fogeys left."

"Just me. Just gas money."

"Well hell, *just* getting you away from corrupting our youth with that *virtues of shoe-leather* bullshit of yours is reason enough, but..."

She's looking through the massive briefing room window as she speaks, scanning the office floor. There's a large number of assigned cubicles. They all contain personal effects but less than a third have people in them. Occupied cubicles display pictures of grandkids. Deserted cubicles display pictures of newlyweds and budding families.

"They're out there," Bart says to her, sympathetic, a doggedness on his sleeve. "In the cold, maybe, but they're here."

Lorre looks to him in earnest. "Bring 'em back, Bart."

3
EMINENCE GRISE

We're in a home office. Out the window of the office is a nice sunny day. To the right of that sunny day is a desk. Against the desk sits a desk chair, its back to us.

"You know, I wonder..." It's a woman's voice.

The wall to the right of the desk chair is adorned with certificates and diplomas. The office also has one of those faux fireplace mantles that contains a space heater and a little light that flickers through a translucent plastic molding of a fire.

"I really do..."

On top of the mantle sits all the photographic evidence necessary to prove that *Kim* and *Marty Koval,* the occupants of the house that houses this office, are in a loving marriage.

"What's that Kimmy?" Bart asks.

To the right of the fake fireplace sits Kim, office proprietor. As said, she's married to Marty, who you might know better as the missing ops team member, Nike 2. Marty and his team have been missing for over two weeks now.

Kim's lounging in an easy chair in full recline. She's looking blankly off at nothing in particular. Her eyes are puffy. Her nose is red and raw.

"I wonder," she repeats. "Should I sit here, in this horrendous comfort with nothing to distract me from the emotions I'm feeling? Or move my boney ass to that torture chamber of an office chair and let the pain in my coccyx offset the grief I feel for my husband?"

Bart shifts in the arm chair he sits in. He's poised now... "Kim, statistically-"

"I know. Your guys made it more than clear. Cults don't kill, they indoctrinate. Terrorists advertise it. Kidnappers ask for ransom..." Blank look becomes significant of emotion. "I also know that if he were still alive, nothing on this earth would have kept him from coming home..." She chokes up a little. Bart moves to her.

"Real paradox isn't it?" She says.

He picks her up and hugs her, then pulls back, looks her in the eyes, "He's just taking the long way home, Kimmy girl."

Kim sniffles, nods in a direction other than any that would put her in the path of Bart's imploring gaze. "Well that makes that real consistent, now..."

She latches back on for a real hug. He consoles her.

"Bart, you need to do me a favor."

"Anything."

"They said there were no traces of blood where Marty was taken." Her tone's a little more professional... "He'd never go down without a fight." More and more professional as she goes... "He's alive... H-he's alive." She says this a second time like she's demanding it of the universe... "But there'd still be blood. They're using that substandard luminol. Won't pick up a damn thing in the dirt." She breaks away from any further consolation now. All business. "Go to my lab, get the trisodium nitrophagic acid from my assistant. If there really was no struggle, the Trinite will be its betrayer. Then, if there really was no struggle... Then... Then I don't know. And that's the point. We'll know we don't know what we're dealing with.

"Real good Kim," Bart says in the furthest thing from platitude. He was counting on this. He's indebted. "Count on me, huh."

She nods.

Bart has a Columbo style *one-more-question* change of demeanor. "Kimmy, anything in the house to defend yourself with?"

"Yeah."

"Keep it that way."

"What are you thinking?"

"That's the problem, all paradox like you said. Two and two keep summing to five... or anything *but* four. Can't be too careful in chaos."

"I'll be careful," she says. "Now, if you excuse me, I think I'm ready for my office chair."

She hugs Bart a last time and he heads for the door.

4

DOWN ON THE FARM

Bart tools along the dirt road leading to the compound where Marty and his team were taken. It's an honest to goodness dirt road, not gravel. People often say they drove a dirt road when, really, they drove a gravel one. Gravel roads are made of gravel. Gravel roads are not dirt roads, therefore. They're gravel roads. The road Bart drives is pure loam, flanked tightly by forest.

Forest eventually opens into the clearing that houses the compound. The agent angles off into the grass at the right of the road, hugging along the bush. He parks.

He exits jangling his keys. *JANGLE! JANGLE! JANGLE!* He jangles on until he's got the key he wants in his fingers. He opens the trunk with it and pulls out a large tank. It turns out to be a pump and nozzle for applying various types of sprays.

He walks toward the compound entrance, pumping the plunger on the tank as he approaches. From his point of view all he sees is the small agrarian operation through the gate of the chain-link fence. Everything's as lush as ever despite no one tending to it.

His pumping is facing more and more resistance, when...
PSSST!
A bit of air and fluid start seeping out of the now pressurized appli-

cator. Bart reflexively tightens the nozzle while not breaking any of his stride. Still futzing, he crosses through the gate of the compound fence.

The nozzle tightened to sufficiency, he looks up again. Tank slips from his grip. He marvels. It's horticulture for miles. A lot of miles. Too many miles. More than could ever be contained in that small acreage. Other than the longhouse, everything's infinite salad.

He reacts to the surreality by shaking his head. He comes back to his senses but it's those damn senses that are giving him the surreality to begin with... Maybe he'll just ignore it? He trunches on, heading to the end of the potato patch nearest the longhouse.

He arrives, stops, and without missing a beat... *SPRITZ! SPRITZ! SPRITZ!* He gives the soil and nightshade leaves a good dousing with Kim's Trinite.

THE CHEMICAL HAS HAD TIME to dry on the soil and nightshade. Nothing's illuminated though. Bart takes out his phone.

He's texting. Phone screen reads,

> Nothing.

BLIPPIDY BLIP! A response.

> Nothing.

> Kimmy: Where'd you look?

CLICK CLICK CLICK...

> Nothing.

> Kimmy: Where'd you look?

> Last known location.

BLIPPIDY BLIP!

> Nothing.

Kimmy: Where'd you look?

> Last known location.

Kimmy: Outta the field too long. Check points of cover...

A look like, *Duh*, on Bart's face. *CLICK CLICK CLICK...*

> Nothing.

Kimmy: Where'd you look?

> Last known location.

Kimmy: Outta the field too long. Check points of cover...

> Outta shape.

SPRITZ! SPRITZ! SPRITZ! HE SPRAYS a tree stump, longhouse perimeter, shed... hell, even a raspberry bush. Everything that a scrambling soldier could hide behind gets a good soak.

HE MOVES TO WHERE THE last of the chemical would have dried. *CLICK CLICK CLICK...*

> Still nothing.

BLIPPIDY BLIP!

> Still nothing.

> Kimmy: so, what are we dealing with?

CLICK CLICK CLICK...

> Still nothing.

> Kimmy: so, what are we dealing with?

> ?

Then...
CRUNCH, CRACK!

Sounds like a twig snapping under a heel. Somebody other than Bart is moving about. Not alone. The agent's eyes go narrow. His movement remains steady. He puts his phone away like a person having just told his wife he'll pick up take-out on the way home.

His left hand inches closer to the Glock holstered on his left side. Fingers get just close enough to feel the heat of the strap of the leather holster when... Change of tack. He moves his left hand across to his right side. Holstered on that side is a taser. You can tell by its yellow handle.

He's drawing it out slowly when...

"I'm not trying to sneak up on you, Bart. We just happen to be in the same place at the same time facing the same direction. By necessity, at least one of us is out of the other's line of sight..."

Taser slips back into the holster with no hesitation at all. Bart turns to face his interlocutor at a reasonable pace, at a reasonable face.

"Here to make up for getting your team captured?" he says to Sim *AKA* Kool-Aid.

Sim stands, pensive, looking conservatively nondescript save for a half-pack pouch slung over his left shoulder and situated at his right breast. Sim is *always* deadpan.

"This is a test of yours. I read your file as soon as I heard you were investigating the disappearances. You're attempting to gauge both my level of competence and temper by insinuating that I've performed poorly. I pass the test if I say - calmly I might add - *you saw the same data I did and would have shared the same intelligence if in my position.*"

Sim's eyes narrow.

Bart smirks. "What else can you tell me? Based on your research, of course..."

No hesitation. "You work alone of late, unusual for you, but you're no misanthrope, so I'm uncertain as to what explains this change."

"I love people Sim... Love 'em. But I call the shots. Alone's easiest when everyone's got to follow my orders."

"Or, it's the fact that on your last two field assignments you were written up for key lapses in judgment, almost certainly at the behest of concerned members of your team. I would assume these lapses due your tendency towards *obsessional neuroses*. Combine that with age-related cognitive decline, highly common in *sixty-*"

"I thought you said you didn't know why I work alone..."

"I said I lacked *certainty* not that I lacked confidence in a hypothesis."

No nonsense from Bart now. "You're in this, you have to do as I say."

"No."

Bart cocks his head but otherwise remains cold at the defiance. He looks at Sim with an *is-that-so?* expression. "Is that so?"

"Indeed. I'm needed on this operation. To be *less* precise, someone who serves the function I do is needed and I'm the only one who serves that function at present. But, you won't refuse. Your psych files indicate that you're not confrontational. At worst, you may apply passive-aggressive tactics in the hope that I just... *leave*."

"Or, maybe I apply *aggressive-aggressive* tactics for a change..."

"Yes, like that exactly. More insinuation. Your insinuating that you will cause me harm is an attempt at making me feel threatened. You're *aggressing* my leaving through indirect language, hence passive means. *Passive-aggressive*... I'm going to collect some soil samples. These aren't tubers common to the region." Sim walks away.

Bart looks blank, then... slight epiphany. "Sim, you only said no to *having* to do as I say, but not *having to* is different from not *willing to* isn't it?"

"*Precisely, Bart.*" is heard off in the distance.

FROM ACROSS THE HIGHWAY WE see Bart pulling up to his room at a local motel. He exits his car and approaches the door. He enters.

Night night.

NEXT MORNING. A LITTLE MISTY and overcast. Same view. Mostly trucks and semi-tractor trailers zip along the highway between us and the motel. They kick up a dirtier oilier heavier sludgier mist. Bart exits his room and walks towards the diner attached to the motel. He enters.

5

TATER

Bart sits at a booth looking over his notes and nursing a cup of coffee. *DING!* goes the bell over the diner door. He looks up just in time to see Sim entering.

He watches from across the restaurant, assessing his prospective partner. What he observes is Sim holding something that looks like a football under one arm while he talks to the cashier. He points at a cookie jar next to the till. Cashier responds and Sim shakes his head *no*. He puts a hand on the cookie jar and says something in response to the cashier. Cashier looks confused. Sim continues talking, face clearly deadpan even at a distance. Cashier shrugs then nods as Sim hands over some cash. He puts the cookie jar, cookies and all, under his free arm and starts walking towards Bart.

He walks right past, slowing just enough to plop the football-looking object onto the table.

THUD!

Bart narrows in on the object, his expression teetering on the edge of a losing neutral. Object's a potato. A really big potato.

Sim returns with the cookie jar. It's *sans cookies* and two thirds full of water. He sets it next to his potato. He swipes a couple sets of silverware from the adjacent booth, and sits opposite Bart.

"Down on the farm again?" Bart asks. "Anything new besides the spud?"

"Soil composition is normal for the region." Sim starts unravelling the napkin from the roll of silverware. "However, it is inadequate to grow the types of horticulture we observed. Strain typings of flora came back inconclusive as well... Are you going to use this?" He's gesturing to Bart's butter knife.

"Just the spoon," Bart says holding up his cup of coffee. "All typings?"

"*All*," Sim say's snagging Bart's knife. "Could be some new recombinant strains in development." Sim tips the tater on its end and jams a knife into it at a 45 degree angle. "This would explain both the robustness and why the typings were inconclusive." He spins the tater 90 degrees and jams another knife in it.

"Something tells me our commune friends only eat organic."

Sim jams another in.

"Have you ever observed any of these purported cultists directly, Bart?"

"I've seen exactly what you've seen."

Jams a fourth.

"Then nothing with your own eyes. Has anyone?"

"Farm supply dealers say there's been no one out of the ordinary making any purchases," Bart says.

Sim lowers the potato into the water of the cookie jar, propping it up on its knife legs.

"Grow operation that big requires a lot of supplies," Bart continues. "Yet nobody saw anyone unusual?"

"Cultists near invariably send friendly innocuous representatives into nearby towns to ingratiate themselves to those communities," Sim adds. "This absence is definitely an anomaly." He's reaching for something. "There's also this...." he pulls a wad of fabric out of the front pouch of his sling pack and unfurls it. Lays it on the table.

"What's that?"

"*That* is a non-regulation sixty-five-percent cotton, thirty-five-percent polyester wide-brim boonie hat in an *operational camouflage* pattern. It was worn by Marty Koval the night of his team's disappearance."

"Where'd you find it?"

"Marty's last known location. The potatoes."

"I wouldn't have missed that."

"Neither would I. Someone involved has been there in the interim."

Bart sighs a thoughtful sigh. Looks to Sim. "We're not dealing with a bunch of eunuchs looking to hitch their wagons to a shooting comet now are we Sim?"

"Doubtful."

Bart shakes his head now. His look reverts back to subtle mystification. He shakes his head once more like he's changing his mind with his face. He's settled on something definitive.

"I've been meaning to check in on Kim. She should know about this." He snags the boonie, slipping out of the booth, reaching for his raincoat as he does. He starts for the door.

Sim unzips the top of his sling pack. He pulls out a cookie previously held in the cookie jar and starts eating it apathetically. He must really be enjoying it...

Then...

"Well, come on if you're in this," Bart yells after him.

Sim's activated by this. He leaves the half cookie on the table, grabs his potato, and slips out the booth.

6

MINIMAL LETHAL

Bart and Sim sit side by side on a small couch in Kim's living room. The cookie-potted potato sits on the coffee table in front of the pair. Curiously, some sprouting has already begun. Sim is eating another cookie. They're both listening to Kim's assessment of the pair's evidence.

"I'll probably pull nothing off Marty's hat but pesticides and potato bug feces, but I appreciate you letting me work this up myself."

Sim looks to Bart in realization, then back to Kim. "*Eminence grise*," he mutters.

"What?" Bart asks.

"*Grey eminence*," Sim clarifies. "An advisor who works behind the scenes and without formal recognition... But I digress."

Kim and Bart look to each other then back to Sim.

"You don't digress," they say in unison

"Be that as it may, I'm going to change the subject... This tea, though far too warm, is very pleasing to the palate."

"How's the cookie?" Kim asks, short.

"Dry."

"I can tell by all the crumbs..."

"Alright alright!" Bart redirects. "Focus you two! Kimmy, look, we don't want to be getting our hopes too high but we know damn well Marty's hat was no accident."

We see that Kim has taken to absent-mindedly caressing the hat, lovingly. It's her husband's after all... She catches what she's doing and immediately stops. It's evidence after all...

"Suspects are trying to communicate with us," Bart adds. "To what end..."

As Bart continues thinking out loud, something strange is going on with Sim. His up to this point unfaltering attention has drifted from the conversation. He's fixating on an object across the room.

...I don't know.

The object is a pedestal for an outdoor weather station. Its display features indoor/outdoor temperature, humidity, current wind speed, gusting, rain gauge, the works. Sim is focusing specifically on the indoor temperature reading.

But they have no leverage if they have no...

Indoor temperature reading is flashing off and on. A change is pending? The reading goes from,

$$23.1°$$
$$\text{to}$$
$$23.5°$$

...hostages.

Sim looks to the window. Window's closed and curtains are motionless under a floor vent. He looks back to the pedestal. It's flashing again as Kim responds to Bart.

Maybe we need to read between the lines, so to speak...

Indoor temperature goes from:

$$23.5°$$
$$\text{To}$$
$$23.8°$$

...Forensics on the hat could get us more of their 'message'.
Sim focuses on Kim and Bart once more.

"We can only hope Kimmy," Bart smiles. "I'm optimistic if you are."

"The only thing keeping me going..." Kim says.

"You can keep Liz and I going this Sunday with those culinary skills of yours..." Bart intimates.

"You putting me to work?" Kim chuckles.

"Just providing the artist a canvas."

"For Liz then, hungry man."

"Then it's a date."

Kim's look turns a little wistful. "Thanks for this."

Bart rises abruptly. Sim emulates this.

"Well, gotta get back at it."

Kim rises in response. "Same."

Sim nods at the two of them, slightly pleasant look of agreement on his face.

Bart reaches out and takes both of Kim's extending hands in his. "Here's to hoping, Kimmy girl."

THE PAIR WALK TO BART'S car outside Kim and Marty's. Sim is minding his tater-in-a-vat as he goes. He's also exercised by Kim and Bart's sociability.

"You just demanded she cook for you."

"Hell Sim, she's a literal chef, degree and everything." Bart wrenches on the car door.

"Of which, you're taking advantage."

"If fishing would take her mind off things, I'd take her fishing." Bart's paused entering the automobile. He's leaning on the side of it, elbows on the roof. "What do *you* do to take your mind off of all that's going on?"

Without missing a beat... "Horticulture."

Bart looks down to the potato and scoffs. He enters the car. Spud's sprouts are even more numerous and elongated, by the way. He sits, waiting for Sim to get in too. He wants closure on this discussion though. "No, Farmer Joe, I mean, what is your primary occupation outside of work?"

Sim seats himself. "Horticulture."

"For more than the last few hours..." Bart says in growing frustration.

"Computational linguistics," he says, pulling at the door.

"Well, color me surprise-"

SLAM!

"Don't change your demeanor as I speak to you Bart. Understand?"

He does. "I do."

"Does Kim have any pets?"

"No."

"There's somebody in the house with her."

"You sure?" Bart asks in all absoluteness.

"It's twenty-point-four-degrees outside. It was twenty-one-point-one-degrees inside Kim's when we arrived. No windows open. No climate control. Start driving and circle around the block."

Bart puts the car in drive and starts it moving.

"We came in," Sim continues. "Temperature increased to twenty-three-point-one-degrees in the living room. No serious fluctuation for nine minutes, then a gradual increase to twenty-three-point-eight-degrees. That puts either a smaller body in the living room or a body our size in an adjacent room. Stop here."

Car stops in front of a fenceless house across the back alley from Kim's.

"Sure? You're Sure?"

"This is something you should bet on."

BART AND SIM BURST OUT of the car and move swiftly through the front yard of the fenceless house. They head around the side, and through to the backyard.

Crossing the alley and into Kim's backyard, Bart pulls his taser.

"Minimal-lethal."

"All I carry."

Bart breaks away from Sim and heads to the left of the rear of Kim's house.

"Wait for me to get around front and we go in together."

Sim nods. Bart disappears around the side. Sim pulls his taser, when...

KIM'S SCREAM! is heard from inside the house.

SMASH!

The front door's been kicked but not opened. Bart's wasting no time now.

Sim tries turning the backdoor knob. It's locked. There's another *SMASH!* This time followed by the *THUMP!* of the swinging front door hitting the adjacent wall. Bart has breached. No time to coordinate. *SMASH!* Sim's through the backdoor.

SIM LOOKS IN ALL DIRECTIONS. It's the kitchen to his left, dining room to the right, hallway in the center. He heads down the hallway, loping briskly along it. It leads straight into the living room but T's off perpendicular to the master bedroom and bath.

Sim hangs a right just as a piercing white light explodes from around the bend. All he can see is Bart rushing into the bedroom, arm over his eyes to protect him from the blinding light. He disappears inside.

Kim!

SWOOSH!

Sim flies, angling into the bedroom so fast he has to go limp into the door frame just to avoid smashing through it.

"Bart!"

Bart's keeled over on the floor, rubbing his eyes.

Sim latches on and helps the agent rise. Bart blinks wildly trying to get his sight back, not easing up until he can see his surroundings sufficiently well.

"She was here," he mutters in disbelief. "She's here!"

Kim and Marty's gun lays on the bed of the otherwise empty room.

7

NOT GONNA LIE...

Bart barges into Lorre's office, Sim in tow.

"They're taking civilians now!"

Lorre makes herself rigid in her chair, poised. "We don't know that yet."

"They took Kim Koval."

"And Kim Koval's been doing everything but drawing a CSIS paycheck. This isn't outside their MO."

"Like hell!"

"*This isn't outside their MO, Bart.*" Lorre says this in recitation. She's up and moving to Sim. She pushes him out the office door and shuts it on him in one fluid motion. She turn's back to Bart in reproach, speaks in a hush. "I don't know if you noticed, but ever since the public caught wind we couldn't stop a few Moonie kidnappers, the Prez and PM have been *just* itching to implement that *emergency* legeslation of theirs."

"I don't know if you noticed Dana, but this *is* an emergency..."

"Listen to you!"

"Maybe just a one-and-done with the *EA*? Send in the heavy artillery and get our people back. One-and-done."

"Except that's not what's going to happen and you know damn

well that's not what's going to happen! It'll be soldiers in the streets and a spook at every dinner table and that's a solution to nothing and that's a solution to nothing in perpetuity."

"Dana..."

"*Nothing*, Bart."

"Goddamn it..."

"Goddamn it what?" she asks.

"Goddamn it you're right."

Lorre sits herself back down and calms. Looks at the agent as though there may just be hope yet. "For your sake, I'm glad to hear that."

A thoughtfulness washes over Bart. The mutual repudiation seems to have had a calming effect. He's deliberating now... "When do you meet with committee?"

"Friday after next." She's got a slight grimness all-a-sudden. "I won't lie to them if our laws won't fix this."

"Sim and I have a few moves left."

"Won't lie."

Bart slides into one of the office's two guest chairs. He holds his tilting head up with the index and middle finger of his left hand, trying to figure out what exactly those *moves* are...

8

VANISHING ACT

The makeshift hunting stand sits like a treehouse for do-it-yourself carnivores. Only, Bart and Sim aren't hunting. At least not in the conventional sense. They sit facing the agrarian compound from the south, at about two-hundred yards out. Various types of binoculars and scopes are strewn about. There are some food wrappers, couple thermoses. Sim's potato's present, hairier than ever.

Stakeout's been going on a while.

Sim's finishing eating a cookie. He's looking pensive, even for him.

"What do *you* do to distract yourself from all this?" he asks Bart.

"Fishing."

"So, your example the other day was autobiographical."

"Damn right. Wife and I have a cabin just over the border. She's there now and I'll be joining her when all of this abduction business is said and done and we have the receipts." Bart has a look of realization. "Do you have any family in-country?"

"No. They're all elsewhere."

"Well, get *anyone* you care about out of here until this *Act* nonsense is off the table. Plenty of room at the cabin."

You'd almost swear Sim looks a little charmed by the casual swiftness with which Bart offered up his house and home. "Thank you, Bart."

"Don't mention it," he says, holding up his field glasses. They're at his eyes but he's not looking through them. "What are we dealing with here Sim?" He sounds almost contemplative... "Ghosts?"

Was that *ghosts* line just some flippancy so Bart could steer clear of any heavy existentialisms? Maybe. Maybe not. What business does a fed like Bart have getting philosophical anyway...

Sim nevertheless finds the right middle-ground... "If we keep ruling out the simpler of consistent explanations, *ghosts* may just be the only explanation we're left with."

"Sim, I didn't take you for a spiritualist."

"The set of things I take to exist grows with every phenomenon I can't explain by appeal to the elements already in it."

Bart chuckles. "Huh?"

"If we can't answer the question, *what's going on?* by appeal to the physical, we'll have no choice but to appeal to the non-physical, what is colloquially referred to as *the spiritual*.

Bart looks a little dire at Sim now. "But we're not there yet?"

"Not yet."

Bart nods, satisfied, looks back out into the distance. "*Rosabelle believe...*"

Sims eyes narrow. "I must admit Bart, I am at a loss as to what that expression means."

"Harry Houdini. Never believed in the spiritual. Neither did his wife, Bess. Nevertheless, they made a promise to each other, should there be an afterlife, then whoever died first would try their damndest to contact the other from beyond the grave. To ensure no trickery, and that the source of contact be no one other than Harry or Bess, they came up with a code phrase that only they would know. Something only the pre-deceased could and would say to the survivor... *Rosabelle believe.*

"I see-"

A flicker of lights in the compound. Bart and Sim snap to it. Both on their scopes.

"Anything?"

"Nothing, just the... Wait... A figure in the corn."

Bart can just barely make out a head and shoulders bobbing and weaving about the Northwest corner of the field.

Just as Bart's about to get a fix on the entity a blue light emits from... Him? Her? Light's beam swaths back and forth across the corn closest the figure. Stalks split the beam out like fingers. They reach as far as they can but the flora is too dense. It's just blue fingers dying in occlusion, resurrected every so many passes as the light angles upward into the night, riding the particles of the atmosphere into the sky.

"I got you now..." Bart says through grit teeth.

The obsession in his tone causes Sim's deadpan to fade a little. It's concern. Subtle, but it's there.

Bart bursts upward, moves for the ladder leading out the stand.

"Bart! You know it's almost certainly a trap," Sim admonishes "The pattern's identical."

The agent pauses his descent. "I'm counting on it."

Sim tries to follow. He's stopped. His leg's cuffed to the bolt-on bench on which he sits. Bart see's Sim struggle.

"I'm sorry Sim. You're needed here."

"That is tactically an error. I'm the only person capable-"

"The last thing I want is one of your rationales."

"You are not qualified-"

"Sim!"

Sim relents. "Then just tell me why."

"*Rosabelle believe.*"

Bart's gone.

WE'RE OVER BART'S SHOULDER, FOLLOWING along behind him. It's like a virtual redo of Marty's team cantering toward the longhouse. Only now we're following just one *very* dogged *very* obsessive sexagenarian.

. . .

SIM SITS CALMLY, SURVEYING HIS surroundings. Scanning. Scanning. Then...

He picks up the plastic garbage bag that he and Bart were using for trash and dumps out the contents. He smooths the plastic then begins folding it over and over again until he has a one-third *by* two *by* eighteen inch strip. He wedges the plastic strip between his ankle and the metal shackle.

So far so good.

He unholsters his taser, pulls the cartridge chunk off the tip and starts submitting the chain of his cuffs to the stunner's voltage.

BART'S THROUGH THE COMPOUND GATE. Even in his single-mindedness he has to take a second to adjust to the surreal immensity of its inside contrasting with the quaintness of its outside.

The agent's focus returns to the figure in the corn. His canter speeds to a thumping jog.

The strange figure, dark and amorphous save for the slight blue tint caused by device-in-hand, appears to catch sight of Bart. Second the figure does, blue tint becomes white flash. Figure's bathed in the piercing brightness, *obscured but present* like in the dark of the night, only now, obscured by seemingly all the light in the world.

Evening's been feast or famine for Bart's retinas...

The figure begins to dematerialize.

"That's right, you pretend to run now!"

Bart's all-out sprinting towards the figure when...

Something halts him. A similar white light bathes him now. Did the light stop him or did he stop himself in the presence of the light? He welcomes it with arms to the sky.

He starts to dematerialize too, only the process is taking longer than it did for the figure. Figure's completely vanished but Bart's dematerialization seems to be hesitating. He notices, disquieted, as...

Sim pops up behind him, stunner in hand. He puts it into the space between Bart's neck and shoulder, *BZZZT!* Dematerialization reverses as Bart crumbles.

White light is on Sim. He looks down to the fully rematerialized Bart.

"*I'm* sorry."

Naturally, it's Sim who's dematerializing now.

Bart looks on, immobilized. "No."

SWOOSH! Sim is gone.

"*No!*"

9

INVOCATION

Lorre sits at a long oak table in one of those impossibly wooden parliamentary hearing rooms. Wooden in terms of structure *and* humor... She's getting soft-boiled by a bunch of pencil-necks who think they're grilling her. Been going on a while.

A Senator hunches toward his microphone. Documents he'll never read are held in one hand, pen he'll never write with is held in the other. He has his reading glasses half down the bridge of his nose forcing him to angle his head back to an absurd degree in order to not read those documents.

"Do you *ultimately* accept responsibility for the many catastrophic errors committed by operatives under your command?" Senator asks, then adds, lightning quick, "Just a *yes* or *no* will suffice."

"No."

"You *don't* accept responsibility?" the Senator says, a little too energetic.

"No," Lorre responds. "I don't accept that *just a yes or no will suffice.* Your loaded questions mean no question at all. There wasn't a single catastrophic error, let alone *many*."

Committee Chair pipes up, indignant. "Ms. Lorre, this committee will be the judge of what is and isn't a real question."

"No it won't," Lorre says in a hush. "People with good sense will..."

"Excuse me?" the Committee Chair says in faux shock.

Lorre shakes her head, looks defeated. Looks the way she looked coming through the door, but the look fit then and the look fits now. She *has* added to her defeat a sense of nothing-left-to-lose, however. She straightens her posture.

"You know, convention dictates that when we come into these *lampoonings of the concept of formality* we extend to you our utmost respect. Yet, in so doing, we're only continuously and futilely extending that respect to a group of people so cosmically inept they couldn't muster the conversational decorum of an ass crack flappin' in a popcorn fart. I've given you, all told, one and a half hours worth of my respect. No more."

The limited audience to this hearing, themselves decorous, nevertheless emit a collective murmur at this. They can't help discuss what was just said.

Though it was only a murmur... "Order! Order!" shouts the Chair.

Rise! Rise! Oh mighty sun!

Things quiet down.

Committee Chair looks gravely at Lorre. "Ms. Lorre, I have every mind to-"

"Madam Chairperson..." faux interrupts the Senator. "Madame Chair... I apologize for interrupting you, and I whole-heartedly condemn such blatant disregard for the sanctity of these proceedings - as I'm sure you do too - but, for the sake of not allowing any further attempts at derailing this hearing, and allowing the good people of this country the closure they so sorely deserve, I would love to be able to conclude my line of inquiry."

"Of course, Senator," the Chair faux relents.

"Thank you Madam Chairperson." He turns his attention back to Lorre. "Ok Agent Lorre, brass tacks then... Is it not true that we are permitted, nay obligated, to declare a state of emergency and invoke *the Act* if indeed *there is an emergency and there is no pre-existing legislation that allows for the ending of this emergency?*"

"That is the exact wording of the legislation, yes."

"Are *our* people going missing all over the country, without resolution?"

"Yes."

"Does that constitute an emergency?"

"Yes."

"And, is there any existing piece of legislation that will allow us to end this emergency?"

A conspicuous hush now... Maybe it existed prior to this question, maybe not, but we're aware of it now.

Lorre hesitates. She glances over her shoulder.

Bart's looking her in the eyes like he knew where those eyes would stop before she even turned... His look is imploring. He ever so subtly nods. Gesture goes unrequited. Lorre looks back to The Senator. She's still hesitant. She takes a deep breath and leans back into the microphone.

"No."

Dull murmur swells again.

"Order. Order!"

Rise! Rise!

10

EMERGENCY MANAGEMENT

T*he Act* has been invoked.

SEQUENCE ONE: PARLIAMENT BUILDINGS, OTTAWA...

Middle-aged soldiers pour out of armored personnel trucks and onto Wellington Street. They assemble in front of the Centre Block of Parliament Hill. Though the area vacant, most soldiers stand guard holding automatic carbines. Some also move in to permeate all ten floors of the Centre Block, marching all the way up to *The Neo White House* that sits on its roof. The Neo White House is a perfect replica of *America of Old's* White House that used to sit in Washington DC. Soldiers in the White House and the Centre Block stand next to doors looking official. Most soldiers on the ground serve as sentries, while about a fifth of them assume formation and begin marching down Wellington.

SEQUENCE TWO: TWO-BEDROOM BUNGALOW, LONDON (ONTARIO)...

A mother cradles her infant in her left arm while trying to read a document held in her right hand. Document reads,

We are writing to inform you of a hold on withdrawals of funds per the following account:

FAMILY SAVER SAVINGS ACCOUNT (ACCT # ***********7491).

...

Funds will be made available again pending authorization from The Financial Transactions and Reports Analysis Center of Amerika East (FINTRAA).

...

...cannot provide any further details as to when...

The mother cries.

SEQUENCE THREE: CHURCH, DISTRICT OF COLUMBIA...
Police, in full tactical gear, are handcuffing a pastor and several of his congregants. Worshippers are all lined up on the grass in front of the church. Yet-to-be-cuffed hands are on heads, cuffed hands are behind backs.

SEQUENCE FOUR: AGRARIAN COMPOUND (GROUND ZERO), UNDISCLOSED LOCATION...
Soldiers line the outside of the compound. It's now demarcated by a five foot swath. Swath is dyed orange and cut out of the surrounding grass and foliage. None are crossing that line until... A single soldier absent-mindedly backs up just a step onto the orange and is immediately and brutally reprimanded by his superior.

. . .

SEQUENCE FIVE: CITY HALL, TORONTO...

We're looking down on a massive protest from about ten stories up, moving down. As the scene gets clearer, we see that police, from several states over, also in full tactical gear, have formed a human blockade and are pushing back the protestors.

The soldiers are using unfinished wooden batons to crack the skulls of any protestors who get within reach. Some police use rifle butts. Periodically, plumes of vaporized eye irritant burst out at the protestors. Troops on horseback tear around the periphery with abandon, occasionally veering into the crowd according to no discernible pattern. Many are trampled.

It's a sea of waving liberalist placards, in condemnation of the totalitarianism, colliding with violently swung batons. It's not subtle, but it *is* a documentary at this point.

SEQUENCE SIX: CSIS HEADQUARTERS, OTTAWA...

Bart stands at Lorre's desk, reaching around his person. He retrieves the materials of interest and tosses them onto the desk. It's his company ID and his holstered gun.

Lorre pushes them back towards him and pulls a bottle of Jameson from a desk drawer.

Bart slumps in the guest chair closest him.

11

TARRED AND I WANNA GO TO BED

The agent stumbles from his kitchen to his living room. He's holding a tall weeping glass of brown liquor in his hand. He's singing in a slurred, despondent, manner.
Show me zha way to go home... home... home...
He moves to an easy chair and plops down.
I'm tarred an' a wanna go to bed...
Takes a sip.
Our view of him is obscured by the back of the chair. However, we can make out his right arm holding the drink and the fact that it's going up and down up and down slowly draining itself with each hoist.
Hash a glass a beer about an hour ago an' shish gone right to my head...
Sip.
We're circling around the back of Bart's chair, clockwise, coming around to his left side.
His face is expressionless, motionless for a second, then...
Sooooooo! Show me the way to go home... home... home.
There's something curious about that hand of his not holding the drink.
I'm tarred an' a' wanna go ta bed...

Couched in it is a digital thermometer, insulated from the heat of Bart's palm by a torn piece of potholder. Digital read-out indicates,

$$22.3°$$

Readout starts to flash.

Had a glash a' beer 'bout an hour ago an' shish gone ryessh to my head...

Now reads,

$$22.9°$$

Bart downs the remainder of his drink. *BURP!* He gets up again, wobbly, and goes back into the kitchen.

He dumps a little crushed ice in his glass, pours a couple gorilla fingers of whiskey in it, then takes a sip. Looks pleased with himself, as though, *this'll do*. He starts walking back to his easy chair.

He's shuffling *again* and minding his weepy glass *again*. Looks like a man concentrating real hard on drunk work that's a sober man's leisure.

Shuffles, shuffles, shuffles, then...

Spins, quick silver-like, sober as anything. He's spinning and reaching out, grabbing at his quarry. He's caught the apparition that was coming up behind him by the lapels. There's immediate recognition in Bart's face. Shock.

It's Marty Koval.

Bart looks him up and down, disgust building as he goes. Marty's wearing an earthy mint-colored fabric. It's flowing, casual, looks really really comfortable yet formal at the same time. Pajamas you'd wear to the prom.

As unique as the fabric is, what stands out most is the platinum insignia Marty wears around his collar. The insignia consists of a triple infinity loop. Each of the three loops contain a unique shape. In the first is a stalk of wheat. In the second, a house. In the third, a drop of water.

"What's this getup?" Bart asks. The question is somehow both rhetorical and inquisitive. "It *was* a cult…"

Marty smiles, speaks tranquilly. "No."

Bart eases his grip a little. He's as suspicious as ever, but easing into some sort of resignation.

Marty puts a hand on Bart's shoulder. "Thanks for looking in on Kim." He takes that hand off Bart's shoulder and uses it to put three fingers onto his insignia. He depresses all three symbols of the infinity loops at once. A familiar white light emerges.

Marty nods goodbye to Bart and starts to dematerialize.

But Bart's not ready to say goodbye…

He's back in field agent mode. He sees that the white light is concentrating into the three infinity loops. Good enough. He comprehends. He lets go of the lapels and snatches the insignia, breaking it free from Marty's collar.

He backs away, himself now dematerializing.

Marty reaches out for the insignia, but…

SWOOSH!

Bart's gone.

12

NECESSITY IS THE MOTHER...

Bart's in a white out for a moment, then... *SWOOSH!* He's at the gate of the agrarian compound, something lurching him forward. He has just a split second for these surroundings to become recognizable as... *SWOOSH!*

HE REMATERIALIZES AGAIN! WILL THIS be an extended stay? He looks around, taking in as much information as he can before god-knows-what happens. The environment he's in is the contrivance of some sort of intelligence but it's unearthly. To twenty-first century eyes, anyway...

It's an office space that's neither sterile nor homey, just accommodating. The surfaces and fixtures are translucent. Not necessarily steel, nor stone, nor glass, nor wood, but translucent. Almost like they could be made of all of the aforementioned materials but with a coat of light amber just for surface's sake.

There's no information, or information movers, anywhere. No video monitors, speakers, computers, electrical outlets... Just objects that serve *immediate* functions like table surfaces and sitting surfaces.

"You figured it out."

Bart turns in time to see The Inventor walking through the frictionless sliding door of *my* office.

Remember me? Sure, I look to be about forty years older than when you last saw me, but Bart doesn't know that... I'm wearing the same style of earthy robes as Marty, insignia at my collar too.

"You remind me of someone I used to know," I say to Bart.

He's still in agent mode. He looks me up and down. This is a good sign. "Why-my getting the impression you brought me here to audition for *Manson Family: The New Batch*?"

"*Brought*?" I chuckle. "You walked right through our door. For what? The third time now?"

"*Door*? You're squatting on crown land."

"*Crown land!* What a dandy vestige. Your *PM*, he may be a fop but he's no royalty. And your *Prez*, he's a different wax ball altogether." Bart continues looking at me discerningly. *Whoever this guy is, he knows Amerika East politics.* I continue. "Let's pretend there's legitimacy in people staking a claim to land they don't live on. Or work. Or even maintain so that other's might work it some day. Even if legitimacy were the case, we weren't *on* any land, crown or otherwise."

"Nonsense!" Bart scoffs. "I got the goddamn potato to prove it."

"And you can keep it. We've got plenty here."

"Here?"

I wave my hand in front of some amber panels along the office wall. The opacity of the panels dissolves into transparency, allowing a view of home.

"My home. Everyone's home."

Through the windows Bart sees many tall buildings made out of the same translucent amber as my office fixtures. There's also a tremendous amount of *bucolia* all around this cityscape. Trees, shrubs, grass. All flowery or fruity or both.

What he's looking at, if it's no illusion, is no present-day Earth either.

Make no mistake, there aren't any flying cars or holographic images or any other such things, but there is an awful lot of teleporting. People are beaming in and out of existence but, curiously too, many are moving about on old-fashioned automobiles. There are electric scooters, bicycles, the odd sedan, even a monorail system. Oddly, it's like they're using these devices for recreation and less to get from A to B. One citizen hops off a bicycle and teleports away as the bicycle dematerializes too.

Bart walks up to the window and gives it a bap.

I chuckle again. "It's not a video monitor Mr. Bart. As your saying goes, *what you see is what you get*." I look to the agent's hand that did the bapping. I realize he's still holding onto Marty's insignia. I realize something else. "You've also been *getting* a lot more than you've been *seeing* too, haven't you?" An idea comes to mind. "If you have a minute, I can make things a lot clearer for you."

Bart swooshes a finger along the window. He rubs this finger to his thumb. "As many as it takes. *Answers* and *my people*, hook or crook."

"We should start out then..."

13

KLAATU BARADA NIKTO

I lead Bart through one of our train stations. We had to walk to it, no teleporting. Thankfully it was on the same block as my office. It's a similar setting as my office too, only with the added fixtures and amenities necessary for travel by rail.

Many people are milling about. The odd person teleports in. The odd person teleports out. Some do this seemingly just to board a train and travel off somewhere else. I notice Bart staring confusedly at all this.

"We still like to take the scenic route from time to time... for nostalgia's sake."

A woman recognizes me and approaches. She's all smiles and her hands are extended. I reciprocate, extending my hands to hers and we shake in salutation. Curiously, it's the same greeting that Bart uses with Kim, of which Bart doesn't fail to notice.

"Your *good old days* aren't even our *next century*," he says.

"Our nostalgia is essential for you to understand this is no illusion." I smile, pointing at a doorway that's periodically alternating from the default amber translucence to a shimmering aqua blue. "This one's ours."

. . .

BART LOOKS OUT THE WINDOW of the train car. He's gathering as much data as he can, so to speak. The train blasts out of the city limits and into the country. There's an instant lushness.

It was here that I noticed something about Bart's deliberation. Something curious but heartening.

It's ceaseless.

"I admire that of your people," I say.

"What's that?"

"Your incredulity. Your tendency to demand proof." I get one of those *good-with-the-bad* pangs of dissonance in my stomach. "What I *don't* admire is your equal tendency to not know a proof when you see it. Or worse, know it, but not alter your thoughts in the face of it. I'll never understand this."

Bart chuckles. He's a little more relaxed looking at the endless bucolia. A *little* more relaxed...

"Most of the time we're not asking for proof," he says. "We're just delaying being taken down a path of understanding we don't wish to tread. Change is all manner of hard." He pauses, looks a little philosophical, then... "*Give us the gift of fire and the first thing we'll do is burn our clothes to stay cold a little longer...*"

"We used to have that problem."

"And I thought you said you couldn't understand..."

"I couldn't. I never understood it then, and I don't understand it now. Lucky for us, one day this tendency just disappeared."

"How'd you manage that?"

"Not sure we really did. At least not intentionally... We tapped into some instinct that lay dormant in near all of us. Acting on this instinct got us to a point where the only thing we couldn't have in abundance was *knowledge*. It became our only novelty. The only thing of any value, therefore. Thankfully for us, the only thing that *could* be of value happened to be the thing of *greatest* value..."

Bart nods. We both turn to our respective windows now, as though, the cosmos was saying, *let the scene rest a minute*.

Then...

A metal hand grabs Bart by the shoulder! He lurches back in defense.

"*Can. I. Offer. You. A. Beverage?*" the metal man's voice simulates.

He's a 'classic' automaton intended to serve customers like it's *the old days*. It has my people's equivalent of a *Coca-Cola* logo on its chest.

"Jeez. *Klaatu Barada Nikto* metal man!" Bart orders, still a tad spooked. He waves the automaton away *no thanks!*

I look at him, intrigued.

He notices my looking intrigued.

"It's from a movie." he says, trying not to confuse. "A film... Motion picture... *The Day the Earth Stood Still*..."

"Oh I know," I point out. "According to your people, it's required viewing for someone in my position."

"Well, that's reassuring. You reminding them of Klaatu, I mean."

"Is it reassuring, Bart? The extraterrestrials in that movie were nothing but *thugs*. Your word I believe..."

Bart furrows his brow. "What?"

"This is our stop!"

BART AND I TRUDGE THROUGH what appears to be grassland. The foliage is waist high, a little encumbering, but Bart doesn't seem to notice as he's still hung up on what I had said earlier.

"What do you mean *thugs*?"

"Thugs?"

"Thugs. You called Klaatu a *thug*."

"Oh, yes! Mr. Bart, those extraterrestrials were totalitarians and little else. Spying on earthlings, turning the Earth into a compliant police state, fearful of what no earthling had even done yet... and for no good reason.

"*No good!* They were developing nuclear bombs to use outside Earth's atmosphere."

We tromp out of the waist-high grass and into some willow bluffs. The bluffs are about twelve feet high and seven yards across. It looks like we're navigating our way through cotton candy bales the size of your Statue of Liberty's head.

"They had small nuclear arms," I rebut. "That's nothing at a galactic scale. The span of time it would take earthlings to figure out how to maneuver a nuclear weapon outside of the solar system would be inordinately large." I turn to face Bart a second. "Can you even do this now?"

"If we hadn't de-proliferated..."

"You sound almost disappointed." I start walking again and Bart follows. "The chances that advanced beings like Klaatu's couldn't easily intercept such weapons is virtually none. They conquered a child's treehouse for fear of BB guns and tricycles."

We tromp out of the bluffs and into something as high as the grass we'd just walked through, only greener and with broader leaves. Bart is too rapt – and a little indignant - to notice.

"What *should* they have done then?" he asks me.

"If you want my opinion, the more principled response would be *first*, understand the minimal threat the earthlings pose. *Second*, leave the Earthlings to their own devices while easily insulating 'we of the other planets' from any threat they *may ever* but likely *will never* pose.

It is at this point that our topic of discussion converges with the subject at hand. I stop. I get a little more matter-of-fact with Bart.

"Rule number one, *unless all you're offering are options they can take or leave, leave them alone.*"

Bart takes this with all due skepticism but not dismissal. Good. He waits for me to continue the walk, but...

"We're here!" I say boisterously. "Look familiar?"

It's the potato patch of the agrarian compound.

"What the f-"

"Just in time!" I say equally boisterously.

Marty comes bursting through what appears to be a portal of some sort just before the fence on the other side of the compound. He materializes out of nowhere.

"What the f-"

14

INTENTIONS

Bart stares at Marty. Just stares. Not up and down. He's done with that. He's looking Marty in the eyes. Has been for a while.

Finally he speaks. "How they been treating you Marty?"

Marty looks a little disappointed. "Bart, you talk to me like I'm a hostage."

"By the looks of things, a hostage of your own mind."

Marty laughs. "Again with the cult stuff. There's. No. Indoctrination."

"Not quite true, Marty," I admonish. "You've believed everything we've told you so far without question. You should be more critical-"

"And I told *you*, I went with my gut on this one. Never steered me wrong yet." Marty smiles at me in good humor.

"Aren't the two of you cute," Bart chides.

"Mr. Bart," I say, pointing at the gate in the compound fence. "You can walk through that pathway and back into your world any time you want. You can take a step backwards and be here in our world any time too. That's why the pathway is here. That's why we took the scenic route. No smoke. No mirrors. This is what I wanted to show you."

"And *this* is where I try to leave and you offer me something I can't live without, only I gotta move in with all *a'* ya if I wanna live with *what I can't live without*?"

"You already have *it*, Bart," Marty says, as though he speaks of abstractions.

Bart looks at him quizzically. Marty flicks at the insignia half-hanging from the agent's grip. Bart reflexively tosses it back to him.

Marty shakes his head in disappointment again, though he's beginning to gesture in a way suggestive of auspice. He opens his left hand, holding Bart's insignia. He opens his right hand to reveal nothing but a bare palm. With the thumb of his left hand he depresses a single button on the insignia. In his right, a brand new insignia materializes out of thin air. He hands the newly conjured insignia to Bart and puts his own back around his collar.

"Go ahead, try it. Just think of whatever your heart desires most in this world and press the button."

Bart smirks, seriously thinks about it for a second. Then... Face turns to stone. Apathy. He opens his palm and lets the insignia fall to the dirt.

"I work for a living."

"Then work for a *life* Bart, not tokens," Marty implores.

"I will when this caper's blown open."

"What more can we help you with Mr. Bart?"

He turns back to face me. No nonsense. Agent mode. "You've been rounding up our best. Intelligence. Special ops..."

"They came to us."

"Why only the young?"

"That's who you sent. You're here too, aren't you?"

"Gotcha there Bart!" Marty laughs. "What are ya now, sixty f-"

"You're squatting," Bart redirects to me.

"We certainly are not. You're a guest of ours right where you stand. That pathway is immaterial, a *substanceless* portal between your world and ours. Only a fool would call that trespassing."

"Oh, believe me, we have people fool enough..." Marty says.

Bart's still not convinced. "Still functions on Amerikan soil..."

"So you're telling me," I start… "We select the least obtrusive means of revealing ourselves in the least productive region of your massive country, taking up literally no space whatsoever, giving all earthlings who wish it their heart's greatest desires, where you then attack us guns-a-blazing, where in response to that we give those attackers *their* heart's greatest desires, and you think the best course of action, in the face of all this, is to deem us an existential threat?" I take a breath. "Worst case scenario of leaving us alone was free produce for everyone. *Enjoy! But no!* You declare a national emergency! And I thought *our* old-world leaders were bad…"

"Well, in fairness," Marty offers. "Our governments never did take kindly to self-sufficient types just minding their own business between bouts of excessive charity…"

Bart looks a little sullen. A little embarrassed in light of the facts. "I guess when you stack the facts up like that…"

"According to how the world is?" Marty once again chides.

"You're being given *the gift of fire* here Mr. Bart…"

"Not so fast!" Bart protests. "*Part two*. I came here for my people. I've found one. Where's everybody else?"

"Where they've always been, at home."

"Come on…"

"You think because you can't see them, they're not there?" I say. "Where's Marty?"

Bart looks quizzical for about the hundredth time for about a hundredth of a second, then resolve. He spins around to where Marty *was* standing.

Marty's gone.

"Where *am* I?" I ask.

Bart turns back to me. I'm gone too.

"*Boo.*"

Bart spins. Marty's back, big as life.

"We can show you how. It's second nature." I say, still out of Bart's sight.

One last spin for the agent. I'm back too.

Bart's kinda getting it, but just how honest are *we* who are giving it?

"You gotta admit, Bart," Marty says. "It would be pretty hard for the feds to swallow their best agents going missing then showing up days later having solved world hunger and flight delays..."

"And *you* gotta admit," Bart offers. "*An inter-dimensional farmer's market that turns federal agents into ninja hippies* isn't exactly the pulp detective novel twist I was expecting."

"Well believe it." Marty says. "You want a clincher, come by Kim's and my place this Sunday for dinner. She'll cook, I'll eat. Bring Liz if you're even dreaming of getting through the front door."

Bart bends down and picks up his new insignia. He flops it in his hand like he's organizing change.

"Is that a *yes*?"

I feel a need to once again temper things. "Let's hold off on any deathbed conversions just yet, Mr. Bart. Your incredulity is still your friend. But, it's a pretty consistent picture-"

"You might even say, it's an absolutely true picture," says a familiar voice entering the conversation. "But there's still one detail missing. Something you've been deliberate about keeping from us, professor..."

Sim and Kimmy have appeared in the grow op. They're wearing my people's earthy-mint pajamas. Insignias too. Sim *does* wear his ever-present half-pack, however.

"...Your intentions."

Bart looks to Sim without emotion, then turns to Kim. Now he beams. Kim rushes to him. She holds out her hands and greets him.

"He *was* taking the long way home," she says in near a whisper.

Whatever emotions Bart's feeling at present, this fact pleases him.

Marty frowns, however. Frowns at Sim.

"Speaking of incredulity... The ever skeptical Sim!" Marty says this like he's introducing Sim as a talk show guest. He turns with open arms to Kim. "*Bay-beee!*" He moves to her, latching on. She reciprocates warmly.

Sim's eyes narrow at this.

Marty looks back to him, slightly reproachful again. "Can't you see that my wife and I have been here for weeks and have only ever been accommodated? We come and go as we please."

"And from those facts," Sim begins. "I may infer, with equal logical validity, that two hypotheses imply the professor's intentions. *One*, he's building our trust over the long term in order to indoctrinate us for use in carrying out his bidding. His bidding towards, say, pillaging the earth of its natural resources.

"*Two*, he's here to ease us into the waters of limitless abundance as well as security, but also that often incompatible counterpart of security, *liberty*. From there, peace and prosperity.

"Either of these mutually contradictory but theoretically consistent hypotheses imply his intentions. Until we can rule out the former, more dire hypothesis, we must remain wary."

I wonder if they can see how I elate at their bravura? It's surreality for *me* now. Not provoked of otherworldly technologies, but of their civil charitable discourse to an end that lays outside of human pride!

It's my turn to rebut...

"You're testing *us* Mr. Sim," I challenge. "You're running a secondary experiment. That is, *hide some of the inferences you've inevitably drawn and see if I'll fill in the gaps*. Well, why not. Here goes...

"You know it is highly improbable that your former hypothesis be true, that we're ingratiating ourselves in order to exploit you. You know nothing close to our technologies exist on Earth. We're not *from* Earth, therefore. It's near impossible we're even from your galaxy.

"Since this is the case, you know very well that the energy needed to travel here from even the nearest galaxy implies we already have enough resources to run our technologies an arbitrarily large number of iterations.

"It would cost us more of our resources, human resources included, to pillage yours. Such travel would also be quite dangerous for us, as your people's hostility has proven. This leaves your hypothesis of concern highly highly improbable.

"Improbable, not impossible. Although plausible in and of themselves, all of your premises need be true in conjunction too, where, the truth of such a conjunction is far less likely. Therefore, your help in proving the correct hypothesis, one way or the other, would be greatly appreciated."

"How can I be of service?" I offer, happily.

"You can start by just *telling* us your intentions," Bart interjects.

I smile. I admit, I'd be indulging myself in my true intentions just by setting out to prove them. So, I'll say the easiest thing in the world for me to say...

"We're not here to pillage," I begin. "We're also not here to grant abundance, but it's ours to give and yours if you want it. We're here just to get a look at you. Food for thought."

"*Food for thought?*"

I didn't realize it at first, but I was absentmindedly running my finger along my insignia, but... "As I said earlier, Mr. Bart, knowledge is the only thing we can't pull out of thin air. Truth and beauty are the only scarce resources of our world. You can never deplete them, but there's never enough to go around. Knowing truth and knowing beauty, sharing them too, that is why we're here."

Bart remains silent at this. Reverent, maybe, but silent.

Sim not so much of either... "A very poignant explanation professor. Now I'm going to prove it."

He beams away.

15

AT HOME

KNOCK! KNOCK! KNOCK!

Kim opens the door, looks disappointed. "Where's Liz?"

Bart's in the doorway *sans* his better half, holding something in a white box. He shakes his head. He then tilts it towards an armed old man of a soldier *standing-standard* on the street corner. Soldier looks like the fixture that he is.

Bart looks disappointed too.

They both look disappointed together.

Then, Bart raises the object in his hands. "She made dessert."

Kim brightens a little, takes the box. "Come in you're out!"

BART AND KIM TALK AS they walk from the entrance to the dining room. Kim's earthy-mint pajama's are flowing, Bart's in nondescript *sears-catalog-casual* so nothing about him is flowing.

"I was talking to a guy from the lake the other day," Kim says. "Bragging. Said he pulled a pike out of there the size of my leg. He was real cheeky about it too. Looking at my legs saying it. Lucky

Marty wasn't there..." Bart laughs. Kim continues. "I said to the guy, how do you even serve a fish like that? He said hell if I know..." She baps Bart on the shoulder. "You sports fisherman, all the same. Give me a fifth the weight of one of your freshwater barracudas in walleye and I'll make you a pickerel cheek bisque that'll turn your taxidermists to doll-makers."

They're in the dining room just as the anecdote comes to a close.

"I believe you know Mr. Personality here..." Kim says in mock mockery.

Sim's sitting at the dinner table. He's wearing his pajamas too... and half-pack.

"He's been here a while," Kim says, tongue-in-cheek. "You can tell by all the crumbs."

And, ya know what, there really are a lot of cookie crumbs scattered around Sim's place setting...

Bart looks to Sim apathetic. Sim's eyes narrow. Kim notices the tension. She pulls out a chair for Bart and he sinks into it, opposite Sim.

"Well, there now," she says. "I'm going to go into the kitchen and get Marty to start drinking beer with you guys out here so he'll stop ruining my pedaheh in there." She moves towards the kitchen, disappears through the doorway.

Bart's been looking Sim up and down from the moment they were reintroduced. Scanning... Scanning... He reaches into his pocket. He's holding something in his hand now.

"Down on the farm again, Sim?" His face contorts into a wry smile.

He slides his little thermometer across the table, the one that helped catch Marty. As the device comes to a rest, we see there's an inscription on its back engraved in a pure platinum placard. It reads,

Rosabelle Believe

"Find anything new?"

Like the two men never even left that tree stand...

"It is really quite remarkable, Bart. When they say they materialize objects out of thin air, they're not lying. That is literally what they are doing. They convert matter to energy, energy to matter. They repurpose ambient atoms down to their subatomic elements and recompose them to form anything they please. It's how they teleport. It's how they reproduce amenities. Everything."

"And you believe the mission statement?"

"Technically, the story's yet to be proven, but we'd be fools not-"

"No shop talk tonight fellas," Marty interrupts, exiting the kitchen. He's carrying three Kokanees with him. "This is a *gangs almost all here* affair." He distributes the bottles to each place setting.

Bart looks to his beer. "I see you've broken out the good stuff." He takes a swig.

"Hey! Let it breathe."

THERE'RE A FEW MORE BEER bottles a piece at each place setting. The men are sitting around the table, doing what men do sitting around a table.

"Yeah?" Marty says, like he's got something to prove. "Well don't make me take it out and prove it to ya. Calluses are healed and everything..."

Bart's smirking. "You could have Chet Akins' fingers transplanted onto your hands and you'd still play that thing like a tree falling on a ukulele!"

"You know what? I'm glad you said that, because now I have every excuse in the world to prove you wrong."

Marty reaches under the table. Sim looks intrigued. Bart prepares for doom. Marty yanks an acoustic guitar out from under there! Like he was waiting for this moment all evening.

"*Ta da!*"

"Oh no!" Bart laughs.

Marty stands up and props his left leg up on the seat of his chair.

He puts the guitar on his knee and starts strumming. The chord progression goes *A A A A D D D D A A A A D D D D* ...

Marty's a lot more adept than you'd think. He affects his best Waylon Jennings voice and...

Lord it's the same old tune, fiddle and guitars.
Where do we take it from here...
...
We need a change...

Bart looks to Sim. "We need a change alright..." He nearly mouths these words. Then, out of nowhere... He joins in!

...Naw, I don't think Hank done it this way...

Marty starts soloing, kinda badly, but effectively. Sim cracks the slightest of grins at the two caterwaullers.

Naw, I don't think Hank done 'em this way...

"Take it home!" Shouts Bart.
More of Marty's soloing...
Then...
Kim's hands caress Marty's shoulders. Marty looks over to her like a lovey-dovey buffoon. Kim looks affectionate but imploring and has a hint of *I'm-sorry-to-do-this-to-ya-Waylon* in her expression. Marty gradually stops playing.

"I've got something to show you all in the kitchen."

KIM'S WAVING HER HANDS OVER a finely made serving of pork tenderloin medallions with pedaheh. She's presenting it as though a TV chef is about to come over and give it a taste-test.

"We're going to play a game tonight, fellas. No, not doing our best impressions of people pretending to enjoy Bart and Marty's duets... We're going to play, *Guess the Real Meal with Bill McNeal*."

She grabs a device to the right of her on the kitchen island. I recognize it immediately. I invented it!

"Now, I really really hate to admit this," she continues. "But we're not dealing with a *you can't beat the real thing* situation here. The professor's technology doesn't just replicate food in form, but down to its every last function. Taste included."

She turns on the device and a blue light emits, same as what Bart and Sim saw in the corn field. She waves it over the meals.

"Capture the *blue* print..."

She finishes scanning the plate and sets the device down. No nonsense-like, she looks at the men, her fingers caressing her insignia.

"...And everyone in the network can have *tenderloin medallions ala pedaheh* anytime they want."

Marty looks a little jealous. Kim depresses the wheat stalk on her insignia. Three identical plates materialize around the original.

She ushers the men to the cupboards. Ensures their backs are to her.

"Close your eyes."

They oblige. She starts shuffling the plates around on the counter, mixing them up.

"No peaking, Marty!"

She finishes the mixing.

"Alright, let's eat!"

*Jessi colter and Waylon Jennings' 'Storms Never Last' plays throughout the meal.

THE GROUP EATS, DRINKS, TALKS, and laughs. Sim is even chatty and jubilant in his own unique way. Although we've never seen this before, the naturalness with which the crew enjoys each others' company gives off the impression this *is* just like old times.

Storms never last, do they baby...

THEY SIT, ALL IN QUIET contentment. Plates are empty with napkins furled atop them. Bart is the first to boost himself up from a food-induced slouch.

"Alright Kimmy, who ate the prize portions and who ate the television static?"

"Fellas?" she welcomes all guessers.

"There was absolutely nothing synthetic-tasting about mine," Sim assures.

"Nah Sim, I had the real one," Marty insists. "I've had Kim's cooking more than any of ya..." Kim pokes her finger into Marty's belly. "It's mine."

All look to Bart.

"Now," he begins. "You all know a man with a palate as refined as mine couldn't possibly be mistaken when he says, mine was the *real meal*."

Marty laughs. "Nice try *Jack in the Box*, I can see the mac and cheese powder on your finger tips from here."

Bart twinkles his fingers. "Read 'em and weep."

The men look to Kim.

"Oh, you guys are gonna hate me for this, but..."

"They're *all* fakes!" Bart intercepts.   "They're *all* fakes!" Kim says.

Bart bursts out laughing. Kim follows.

Then...

BANG! CRASH!

A clamor is heard coming in through the open dining room window. Everyone at the dinner table is on instant high-alert.

A SCREAM!

It's coming from Kim and Marty's next door neighbors' house.

Silhouettes are chaotic through the neighbors' curtain-covered living-room window.

"We told you, we weren't even there! Please!" It's a man's voice, coming from the neighbor's house. Faint.

KIM AND MARTY'S DINING ROOM is deserted. All diners have vanished, seemingly into thin air - as they've been taught.

TWO SOLDIERS HOLD AN *ELDERLY* Husband in detention as a third soldier shoves the man's pleading *Elderly Wife* into an arm chair. The Husband wasn't resisting until the second they laid hands on his Wife. He sure is now.

Shoving soldier spins around towards the now struggling Husband. He points his carbine right into the old man's face. Wife screams once more. Husband feels his wife's trauma and relents, goes still.

An *All-Purpose Bureaucrat* oozes onto the scene like he was hiding until the soldiers could detain the scary scary elderly couple...

He speaks at a rapid pace, though rote. "Understand that what I do now I do as an act of grace. I am under no obligation, as per *The Act*, to explain in any detail why you are being detained but I nevertheless will at present. Listen closely as I am not about to repeat myself. You are hereby under arrest on charges of *conspiracy to counsel the commission of mischief* and are to be remanded to the nearest detention facility forthwith."

"No," insists the husband. "I... I've been a lawyer for too many years. I know of no such law."

Bureaucrat smirks. "As per section four-point-eight-three subsection five of *The Act*, the administer of *The Act*, the Justice Minister, reserves special authority to suspend the administering of due process in the prosequent administering of any pre-existing legislation, or any discretionary legislation *which* the administer be permitted to enact it and/or enforce it in the interim in which *The Act* is invocatory... *ARE WE PAYING ATTENTION?*" He let's this last part out in a startling shout. He immediately quiets again. "Did you catch it?"

"Catch what?" asks the Wife, still shaking.

"The error. It was not meant to be '*which* the administer be permitted...' but '*should* the administer be permitted...'. Instead of the conditional, we have the absolute. This phrasing may be in error, but it nevertheless makes explicitly clear that the minister may invent any illegality he wishes. Hence, *conspiracy to commit the counseling of mischief.*

"I thought it was *conspiracy to counsel the commission of mischief,*" the Wife corrects.

"Well," Bureaucrat minces smugly. "It's one of the two now isn't it?"

"You're putting us out on ice flows because of a typo?"

"No. Not at all..." assures Bureaucrat. "There's a typo *because* we're putting you out on ice flows." He smiles a sleazy smile. "Alright, now even my graciousness has its limits. Let's get on with this."

"This is tyranny!"

"Oh come now," Bureaucrat assures. "You live in a democracy... It says so right in *The Act.*"

Bureaucrat waves his hands and the soldiers start dragging the elderly couple out of their own living-room. The wife sobs and the husband once again struggles to get to her. The Bureaucrat notices their trauma.

"Separate vehicles, officers."

Then...

Kim emerges out of nowhere and drives Bart's taser right into the chest of the soldier dragging the Elderly Woman. Bureaucrat spins to see the soldier fall. He goes slack-jawed, shudders.

Then...

Marty and Sim emerge out of nowhere, Marty putting one of the two remaining soldiers in a sleeper hold as Sim tazes the neck of the other.

Bureaucrat spins just in time to see these soldiers fall too. He's white as a sheet now and literally vibrating.

Then...

"What do you think you're doing?" Bart, out of nowhere, grabs Bureaucrat by the throat and drives him into the couch. Once planted, Bart releases him. Bureaucrat sits breathing heavy, eye's darting all around, looking at the scene in disbelief.

Kim leads the elderly couple out of the room and around the corner. Bureaucrat turns to watch this, vibrating but otherwise catatonic.

"Well!" Bart demands.

Bureaucrat's head turns lightning quick back to Bart.

A burst of white light erupts from where Kim has taken the couple.

Bureaucrat's head turns to the light with the same quickness.

SWOOSH!

He jumps at the swoosh.

Bart grabs Bureaucrat by his face and focuses its attention back onto him.

"Justify yourself you little weasel."

He attempts a response. He's still shaking. "Th-th-this is c-c-clear treason! I-insurrection. Terrorists! F-f-f-f-fascists..."

"You were about to throw a grandma and grandpa into an internment camp and you're calling us fascists?"

"T-they broke the l-l-law! A-a-actions have consequences."

"What actions?"

Actions have consequences. Actions have consequences. Actions have consequences...

"Well now your consequences have consequences."

Actions have consequences.

"My god Bart, it's like he has no mind at all," Marty observes. "No free will."

"You're quite nearly correct Marty..." Sim adds.

Actions have consequences.

"...He was selected for his officiousness, but he is only human. The pain he feels perpetuating these horrors is too great a strain..."

Actions have consequences.

"...His rote slogans aren't meant for us in any way. They're meant for him and him alone. He's saying them to quell his dissonance."

Actions have consequences.

"We won't get anything out of him, Bart laments. "Who needs it anyway?" He walks to the window of the living room, focusing on the prisoner transport vehicles out front. "We thought we could just slip back into normal so easily didn't we?" He turns to Sim. "I think I've figured out a way for you to prove your hypothesis."

Sim's eyes narrow.

16

FLIPPING SWITCHES

I sit at my desk, listening to their proposal.
    Bart sits across from me, speaking animatedly. Sim doesn't. He's sitting, make no mistake, even speaking, only *not* animatedly. They've culminated to something...

"Well?" Bart requests.

I mull everything over a second or two, then... Resolve. I hope...

"We are willing to help you in any way you need," I begin. "Save for one, we will not intervene in your world. It's yours, so it's yours alone to maintain."

"You realize," Sim says in a somewhat dire tone. "If our plan comes to fruition, this will mean the immediate depletion, possibly exhaustion, of Earth's resources?

"It's also a pretty good refutation of the idea *my people came to plunder your treasures*, if I'm not mistaken?"

"Precisely."

I smile at this, then rise. "Follow me."

IN STRUCTURE, THE LAB NEXT my office is the same environment as my basement laboratory, that is, a room with many many socialized rats in pens. In terms of the particulars, the key differences are only the updated technologies.

Bart and Sim look to each other like they understand this is a lab running experiments of some sort but, short of this, understand little else.

"You'll have your work cut out for you," I say, approaching a pair of rats tapping away in their opposing chambers. I gesture for Bart and Sim to pay attention as I take a *Spiritual Progeny of Fat* out of his chamber and away from his three-for-one acquisition of resources.

"There are a few of us..." I continue, "...Products of some arcane recipe of instinct and environment, who will never accept what is on offer, no matter what is on offer..."

I bring Fat to the open-concept pen for the recovered rats and put him in. He immediately runs to an unoccupied pedestal and taps it. A single food pellet shoots out. Fat looks disappointed.

"...By accident of a *give and take* relationship where they were the first to *take*."

Fat begins darting from unoccupied pedestal to unoccupied pedestal, looking for that magical three-for-one jackpot of a dispenser. No luck. He's becoming more and more agitated. He looks to the other rats *tap tap tapping* for resources but not sending any of them his way.

Fat goes raving.

At first he hisses at the other rats. They just ignore him. They're too busy tapping and living - more *living* than *tapping*. Fat tries violence now. He charges at *The Nearest Rat* – call him *Nat* - and grabs him by his throat, wringing on it.

Nat manages to break free of Fat's grip and gets some distance between himself and his attacker. He backs up... he stops... he rears... he charges at Fat.

Just as Nat gets within a whisker's distance, he leaps. He flies right over Fat and keeps on running.

Fat turns to chase after Nat, but...

Nat's vanished.

Fat turns back to the other rats...

They've vanished too.

Fat's all alone, as agitated as ever.

Like it's the only *last* desperate move he can make, he starts hoarding as much of the materials abandoned by the other rats as he can. He piles them into a corner of the pen and starts guarding them, hissing in all directions. Hissing at nothing. He starts using his hind legs to fling valuable food and building materials up and out of the pen.

"They're dogs in the manger now. They'll destroy everything and everyone before they'll live in a world of infinite resources... If only because destruction means deprivation for those who dare to no longer function *beneath* them."

Fat's still hissing, panting, raving, running in circles.

"Bart, Sim, you must insulate yourselves from those among you you know to possess such tendencies."

Fat carries on. He's huffing and puffing at greater frequency. He's spent. He needs food and water but he's too bull-headed to consume any. He lays down, exhausted, gasping for air like even *that* he wishes he could deprive the whole world of.

I give a look to Bart and Sim that suggests to them, *you've both seen enough*. I reach into the pen to remove Fat, when...

Bart grabs my hand, gesturing a *don't*.

"Bart, he's dying."

The agent shakes his head at me, looks uncharacteristically imposing... Real damn imposing. I relent.

Sim's eyes narrow.

Bart stands, arms crossed, looking cooly into the pen at the dying rodent.

"This is how we get back our *normal*."

17

LIMITLESS ABUNDANCE

It begins.

SEQUENCE ONE: TWO-BEDROOM BUNGALOW, LONDON (ONTARIO)...
A mother, the same mother who had her account frozen as a matter of fact, holds her infant in her arms. She's entering her kitchen from the dining room. Her countertops have been conspicuously bare. Have been for a long time. Today they're bare save for a single item.

The mother looks closer. It's a triple-loop insignia. A note taped to it reads,

Try Me.

Mom detaches and picks up the note. We see on the reverse of the note additional print too small to make out. She flips it, reads the other side fast and curiously. She picks up the insignia now, closes her eyes, and presses the button...

A bottle of baby formula materializes on the countertop.
The mother cries.

SEQUENCE TWO: CHURCH, DISTRICT OF COLUMBIA...

A large black shuttle van screeches to a halt in front of the church, *Department of Parole* written on its side. A half dozen middle-aged soldiers in full tactical gear pour out of it. Where do these guys keep coming from?

Our recently paroled - *escaped?* - Pastor is preaching to his congregation. He's looking down at his bible when suddenly alerted to the presence outside. His head bolts upright. He goes silent, looking toward the door of the church. The congregants' heads spin backwards to the door too.

Soldiers are preparing to breach the church doors. Command nods. On 3, 2, 1...

BOOM!

Soldiers pour in, carbines at the ready. They halt, look shocked.

Church is empty. Quiet... As... A... Church...

SEQUENCE THREE: CITY HALL, TORONTO...

City Hall grounds look completely deserted, streets too, not even any vehicles. Protest signs and unfinished batons are strewn about, but that's it.

SEQUENCE FOUR: PARLIAMENT BUILDINGS, OTTAWA...

Same situation on parliament hill. No people in sight.

Nothing.

We move over the Centennial Flame, on up around the Peace Tower, and into...

...The Oval Office. We're looking over the shoulder of a stocky man in silhouette, peering out his window at the lack of proceedings.

A slender wisp of a man, also in silhouette, hesitantly sidles up beside stocky-man, joining him in his observation.

SEQUENCE FIVE: *A SUBURB, ANYWHERE AMERIKA...*
    A suburb burns to the ground.

SEQUENCE SIX: *A FARMER'S FIELD, ANYWHERE AMERIKA...*
    A farmer's field burns to the ground.

SEQUENCE SEVEN: *A SUPERMARKET, ANYWHERE AMERIKA...*
    A supermarket burns to the ground.

SEQUENCE EIGHT: *A SUBURB, ANYWHERE AMERIKA...*
    The suburb is back, none the worse for wear.

SEQUENCE NINE: *A FARMER'S FIELD, ANYWHERE AMERIKA...*
    The farmer's field is back, none the worse for wear.

SEQUENCE TEN: *A SUPERMARKET, ANYWHERE AMERIKA...*
    The supermarket is back, none the worse for wear.

18

RATS IN THE MANGER

BOOM!

The Prez barges into The Oval Office, *The PM* in tow.

"They think they can *jush* live without us huh?" Prez shouts, not necessarily for anyone's ears but his... He perches himself back on his chair.

As I said earlier, the Prez is a stocky guy, stockier than the PM anyway. He's in his seventies, has a white wispy comb-over that fools people everywhere but in the light. His voice alters from a badly acted folksy drawl to a raspy marble-mouthed bellow when he talks.

"C'Mon man! Who do they think will put food on their families?"

PM's over The Prez' shoulder at present. He's smarmy, preppy, and frail... about fifty. He speaks with a weak voice, like he's Mr. Haney shouting through a mile of weeping tile.

"What about *uh* our stuff?" the PM worries.

Prez gets a look on his face like he's about to say something profound. "We have a saying down south-"

"Aren't you from *uh'um* Pennsylvania?"

"Don't interrupt me!" He bellows, bolting upright in his chair. "*They* have a *shaying* down south..." He says this a little calmer. He dumps himself back into his desk chair and spins it towards the window. PM rests his hand on the headrest of the chair, looking out the window as well. The Prez continues drawling on...

"*A single ant can live a lifetime off the nectar of the last raisin of the last grape of the last vine of his once great society.*"

"And you're just the bug to do it eh?" says a disembodied voice.

Chair spins. Prez is looking right at Bart. Bart is looking right back.

Prez flips open the face of his watch and starts pushing a little button underneath, repeatedly.

"No one's coming."

Kim, Marty, and Sim come out from behind various objects in the office.

"To save you, anyway."

The PM grabs onto the Prez' wrist device and starts pushing the little button repeatedly. The Prez shakes him off and grumbles something inaudible at him in reproach. He looks back to Bart with a plastic stoicism behind crooked smile and semi-vacant stare.

"What? Here to *petilshun* your government?" A look of recognition comes across his face. "*Yeah*... I know you. Lorre's lapdog." Prez points to the PM. "You two're why junior didn't get his *Urmgencies* Act when he wanted. You're finished. So help me..." He gets flustered. "You know... The *thing*... So help me... *gawd!* I'll have you and Lorre for *treashun!* Yer doooo-oooo-oone!" *An image of Fat hissing at the other rats...* "What the hell do you want?"

"Just to finish what you started..." Bart assures. "*A single ant can live a lifetime off the nectar of the last raisin of the last grape of the last vine of his once great society... He need only stand on the corpses of his brethren to reach it.*"

"But," Kim adds. "Does he destroy his brethren to hasten the *end* of this process, or its *beginning*?"

"And *that* is the question, Kim..." Bart leans back in his chair. "But not for men like these. These men are going to save the world..."

"The whole world?"

"The whole... And for that, they deserve only our pity, never fear."

Bart gets up, start's walking away.

"You're finished!" shouts Prez. "You're under arrest!"

"Pity."

Bart keeps walking. His team follows.

"You stop you bastards!"

They keep on.

Prez bolts upright, starts stomping after Bart... Starts running after Bart.

Bart turns, holds up his hand to The Prez. *Stop, you maniac.* This doesn't deter him in the least. He charges right into Bart...

*An image of Fat wrangling Nat's neck...

...and through him.

Through?

Then...

The PM, thoughtlessly chasing the more powerful politician in the room, charges right into *and through* Bart as well.

THE PREZ BURSTS THROUGH WHAT turns out to be a dimensional pathway that began at Bart and ended in my office.

Now the PM emerges.

"You came," I say. Rather warmly, I'd like to hope.

19

THINK IT OVER

I gesture for my two guests to sit. The Prez immediately moves for my desk chair. He plops himself down, looks to me with a *your move* expression that immediately falters. Prez notices that PM is just standing in place, clueless.

AHEM!

Prez pounds the shoulder of the desk chair he's usurped. PM bolts toward it.

Uhh...

He stands by his boss' side and puts his hand on the corner of the chair. Prez resumes his *your move* demeanor.

I wave my hands. The desk area of the office spins like on a lazy Susan while The Prez' chair morphs into two uncomfortable-looking translucent stools, one of them knocking the PM off balance and onto it in the process. They both sit facing me now in my newly materialized office chair. Prez and PM look uncomfortable by design. Am I being petty?

"We may be accommodating, but we're not pushovers," I say.

Prez looks as agitated as ever. "That's why you've been taking pieces off the chess board I take it?"

"Absolutely, starting with our own."

"And Junior and I are next," Prez says, pointing to PM.

"That's up to neither you nor me."

"Everything is up to me!"

"Collect a tax dollar."

Prez says nothing. Does nothing other than vibrate more aggressively.

"*Uh...*" is the PM's contribution.

Then...

"This is *treashun!*" bellows the Prez.

"The people of a republic have turned their backs to you. Your not leaving them be is what's treasonous."

More indignation. "I didn't get as far as I did by being a political philosopher. The concept of *republic* means nothing to me. I'm a pragmatist."

"Do something useful."

Crickets from the Prez again on this one. Just more agitation.

Then...

"This is abduction!"

"Leave."

"Nobody issues me an imperative."

I smile a wry smile. "Well, since you're now a willing audience... Let me tell you about *our* world..."

I LEAN BACK IN MY chair, hands folded and resting on my midsection. I think I explained things quite well if I do say so...

"And that's it. That's the story."

The Prez and The PM sit in quiet contemplation a second. Then...

"Communist crap!" says The Prez.   "Capitalist greed!" says The PM.

"Ha!"

"What's so funny?"

"We don't seek profits." I begin. "And, we haven't any markets, let alone free markets."

Prez' demeanor shifts. Looks like he's starting to enjoy himself... He turns to The PM. "Told ya Junior! Commies!"

Umm, uh...

"We're no collective either..." I say. "...Acting towards the end of any collective. We're individuals, with plenty of hierarchies, and we *love* our private property."

"Mixed economy *namby-pamby-ness*... Knew it!"

"No."

Prez scoffs. "Guess you're not even the philosopher I thought you were. There's no economies left genius."

"*No economies.* Right."

"What are you talking about?"

"No economy," I say. "*A system in which scarce resources are accumulated and distributed according to more or less efficient methods...* where my world has *no* scarce resources... can have no such system. We enjoy limitless material wealth and you are welcome to enjoy it too."

Prez and PM stare blankly a second.

Then...

"Communist crap!"   "Capitalist greed!"

"Ha! Anyway, in the spirit of diplomacy, I am providing you a complete list of all of the Earthly locations of our pathways."

Prez looks suspicious. PM looks like a doofus.

"What's the game?" asks Prez.

"*Diplomacy,*" I suggest.

"You think we're going to open up negotiations with you?"

"We're immaterial. This is our first and last meeting. I'm merely brokering the opening of said diplomatic relations."

"You're a no good collaborator. Who you in bed with? *ALQ? Charpentier? Romeyo?* Who?

"Being a broker, you in equal proportion... But this relationship is only as political as it needs to be to make it not political. The parties involved are you and the body of *the people* who just want to be left alone."

"They'll get nothing from me."

I lean forward, can't help it. I'm curious about the confidence currently confronting me. Confidence with so little to back it up. I need a closer look at this character. My insistence needs to be made clear as well... So I lean, therefore.

"It's interesting that you think you have any leverage at this point," I say. "The people are not here to ask you for anything. They're here to offer you comfort in your transition. This, as your bureaucrats have been taught to say, is an act of grace."

"How dare they!"

"Your bureaucrats? I agree."

"The hoi polloi!"

"That's their offer. That is, everything you could ever want *but* control. That or nothing."

The Prez smiles a hint of a crooked smile. "*Everything* eh?"

"*But* control..."

I lean even closer, watching the man's wheels turning. What can I say, I'm intrigued.

"What drives a man like you?" I ask.

"Conceptual immortality."

"Then be the first politician on Earth to ever step aside and let life happen. You'll be in the history books forever."

"*Everything*..."

"*But* control..."

Um uh...

Prez leans back, fingertips pressing together turning his hands into a steeple. "Well, naturally, we'll have to think this all over..."

"Naturally."

The Prez bolts up off his stool, dragging PM up by the collar.

"We'll let ourselves out."

"Whatever you please."

Prez pushes PM along towards the other side of the room, the side from which they entered. PM started out not resisting but his posture stiffens more and more the closer he gets to that exit portal. Sufficiently close, he stops the Prez' pushing completely. He looks back, apprehensive. Prez grimaces and gestures a *get in there* hand motion. PM inches into the portal, and...

SCHLOOP!

He's gone. Then... He pops his head back into our side of the portal and nods an *it's safe* nod at Prez. Prez moves toward the portal now, posturing like a real hero despite his previous behavior.

SCHLOOP!

Gone.

Then...

Bart has revealed himself, emerging from behind... or under... or from on top of... something or other.

"So, what do you think he'll do?" I ask him.

"Think this all over..."

20

FOOD, NEST, WATER

Smash cut to...

The last of Amerika East's standing armies are lined up, chock-a-block, in formation, marching towards the compound-gate portal. They're the oldest and the youngest the armed forces have to offer, volunteer or otherwise. They're seventeen-to-twenty-ones and the fifty-five-plus.

Soldiers are following two bulldozers.

"Halt!" shouts the sixty-year-old platoon leader. "Hanson! Samuels! Tear down that fence."

The two soldiers manning the bulldozers split off at the gate and begin tearing through the fence length-wise. They operate like two mechanical stagehands drawing the curtains.

They finish and...

"March!"

...The marching recommences.

The soldiers approach the orange boundary.

WE'RE AT THE OTHER SIDE of the portal, awaiting the marching soldiers' entry.

A bit of a beat...

The first row of soldiers stomp through, then...

TROMP! TROMP! TROMP! TROMP!

Those further behind *tromp* right into the backs of those up front. Soldiers up front have ground to a halt. They're marveling at what lays before them.

It's not the agrarian compound anymore. It's a vast sea of sod, encased in blue sky, going on for miles. It's like a par *one-hundred-eighty-five*. There's an object about fifty yards out from the portal entrance.

"*Maaaa-aaarch!*"

Soldiers regain composure and head toward that object. They get within fifteen feet of it and...

"Halt! Hanson, take point." Hanson does. Leader stays well back and continues barking. "Tell us what we're looking at."

Hanson, looking to be about twenty, hence young enough and naive enough to be perfect fodder, moves cautiously toward the object. It looks to be a small waist-high table. Something's on it. Hanson stops. What he beholds is another triple-loop insignia. This one also has a note attached.

Note reads,

Your heart's greatest desire.

Hanson takes the insignia's taped-on note and flips it over. The opposite side reads,

Press me.

There's a picture of the *house button* under the print.

"What is it soldier?"

"It's a button," Hanson says.

"What kind of button?"

"A button that says I should press it..."

Silence

Then...

"Press it, soldier."

"Hell no!"

"That's an order!"

Hanson's hand drops to his side, a little shaky. We're looking at Hanson's shaking hand as the mechanics inside moving guns are heard moving. *CLUCK-A-LUTCH!* Over Hanson's shoulder we see all other soldiers are holding their guns on him like a firing squad.

We're looking at Hanson's face again, steady as a rock.

We're looking at Hanson's hand again, still shaking.

He takes a deep breath.

He picks up the insignia, closes his eyes, and gives the home button a push. Lights start to emerge from the area just in front of the pedestal, brighter and brighter. All soldiers, including *Platoon Leader*, slowly recoil and put their arms up in protection.

Hanson stands fast.

Brighter, brighter... *SWOOSH!*

Lights are gone.

Hanson's face is stone again. What's he looking at?

It's a house with a *Sold* sign in the yard. It's a modest house, for a young family. You can tell because there are children's toys strewn about the lawn.

Hanson's stony visage softens. A hint of a smile.

21

NORMAL

Soldiers are gone. Spooks are gone. Government-types in general are gone.

People are back though, people of all shapes and sizes, living their lives. They're teleporting like crazy, same as in my world. Otherwise it's just Earthlings living as they would if there weren't countless hapless buffoons everywhere thinking they knew what was best for everyone and that they were entitled to thrust this *best* onto everyone.

It's glorious.

WE HEAR WHAT SOUNDS LIKE the Prez, his figure bathed in shadow, talking to three other figures *just* as shadowy.

"We panic 'em," Prez says. "We panic the extremists, they control the moderates."

"What extremists?" says one of the shadowy figures. "Besides, extremists need leverage, need everyone else to believe their extremism is the consensus. *Everyone else* won't be fooled."

Another figure consults... "You want a critical mass of scaredy-cat whackos to push the disobedient around cuz you've fooled 'em into believing disobedience is lethal? You want pitchfork wavers? You want witch hunts? Guess what? Everyone's fine with witches now since, quite frankly, everyone's a witch! Try to burn 'em at the stake, they vanish and take the stake with 'em."

The third figure recapitulates... "You can't scare 'em this way. The prudes, the puritans, the bigots... They were the first everyone turned their backs on."

"Let's run the panic playbook, then..." Demands The Prez. "*War.*"

"Why would anyone in their position fight a war?"

"Goddamnit! *Famine*?"

"Punitive taxes, induced riots, land confiscation... You burned it all down and they want for nothing. You know this."

"*Pestilence*?" Prez says, a little weaker.

"They don't get sick. They know they don't get sick. They know they won't get sick."

"Tell 'em the hospitals are overrun."

"They've mastered the basic logic necessary to understand that if nobody's sick, then nobody's sick in a hospital..."

"*Death!*" demands Prez, desperate.

"For crying out loud! They've never lived better."

"Not what I meant..." Prez says in a tone more than ominous.

"You can't mean..."

"Just a few executions to make an example of 'em..."

"Enough!" all three shadow consultants say in unison. "You will die before any of them do."

SMASH!

The three figures break to pieces.

The PM flips on the lights revealing a broken mirror in triptych. The last few hanging shards reflect The Prez.

"Who told you to do that!" Prez barks. PM shuts off the lights but not before we catch a gleam of recognition in the three reflecting eyes of what's left of that tryptic. "Back on!"

PM flips the switch again. Light floods the office once more.

There's an object sitting atop a table to the right side of the office door. We hear the Prez' *STOMP! STOMP! STOMPING!* Looking closer at the object, we see a third *Try Me* insignia. The Prez' hand swipes it.

GRRRRR!

He throws it, angrily, smashing the last remaining shards of the tryptich.

SMASH!

THE PREZ, WITH PM IN tow, bursts out onto Wellington Street. People are teleporting in and out of existence - walking, jogging, picnicking, living. All ignore the last two politicians in the world.

Naturally, The Prez doesn't like this. "I'm your commander in chief! I'm your commander in chief!"

All continue to ignore him, so he screams. Just screams. Closes his eyes and let's out a red-faced screaming tantrum.

HE FINALLY OPENS HIS EYES again.

Streets are empty. People are gone.

"I'm your commander in chief..." he says petering out. "I'm... chief..."

Bart appears out of nowhere, still in his Sears casual.

He looks Prez in the eyes. "You Don't know how to handle this, do you? People like you never did."

Prez crumbles, gesturing at Bart with his hands. Could be hostility could be contrition.

WE'RE BACK ON FAT, DYING in his pen as Bart stands, arms crossed, looking cooly at the struggling rodent.

He's dying Bart!

The agent continues to watch as the rodent fades.

Then...

A *Tap Tap Tapping* can be heard.

A rat has materialized at Fat's pedestal and is generating some resources from it. The rat brings her newly acquired food pellet to Fat.

Tap tap tap.

Another rat has done the same. Then...

Tap tap tap.

Tap tap tap.

Tap tap tap.

Tap tap tap...

Finished, the rats go back to living their lives.

It's an embarrassment of riches for Fat, but he still refuses to eat... He refuses to eat because he's dragging himself to the nearest pedestal.

They perish, he perishes. He perishes, they thrive...

He arrives.

He was always a kept little child. A product of their grace...

He arrives, depresses the Paddle, and drinks the dispensed sip of water.

He knows this now...

"I'll be damned."

BART DROPS AN INSIGNIA INTO THE PREZ' outstretched hand. "You better learn to live with yourself if you ever want to live with us," he says. "And you?" He's looking at the PM now.

Uh...

Bart turns and walks away as all who had previously disappeared come back into the open.

We can barely make out over Bart's shoulder, as he walks away, a woman hunkering down beside The Prez.

The agent snaps his insignia into his shirt collar.

EPILOGUE
THE PRIME DIRECTIVE

It's The Inventor's office. Bart's here. He's still wearing his Sears attire, but he's still wearing his insignia too.

"So, what now for you?" he asks.

"I continue what the professor started..." Sim's sitting at my old desk, potted potato plant at the corner of it and cookie crumbs everywhere else. "...Much orientation is required."

"I'm sure you'll do fine, Sim."

"And, what now for you Bart?" I ask, having just materialized.

"Speak of the devil..." Bart smiles at me half in greeting, half in the good humor of all this... "Who was it who said, *When everything you know bores you, know more*? There's a lot to explore, a lot to discover. Gotta keep things interesting."

"Not *so* interesting I hope..."

"How do you mean?"

"I think our meeting all those months back has provided a learning lesson. It's not enough to leave people to *find you*. Some are simply not ready. Unless crossing paths is inevitable, best to stay out of sight."

"I'll put that principle to the top of my list." Bart ticks an imaginary box on an imaginary list. His look turns to one of solicitation. "Kim and Marty are making dinner tonight," he says. "The old fashioned way. Come on by."

"Breaking the rules already?"

"How's that?"

"*Don't hassle the locals.* I don't want to be a bother..."

"On the contrary. You can't be a bother when you're our invited guest. Your absence would be more upsetting."

"Don't think I can argue with that..." I laugh.

Bart turns to The Inventor. "What about you, Sim?"

"Are you asking if I'm coming to dinner or if I can effectively argue against your rationale? The answer is *yes* to both."

"Now Sim, there's a difference between *being able* to make the argument and *desiring* to make the argument isn't there?"

"Precisely, Bart."

"Well then, I'll see you both this evening."

"Bart waves and teleports away.

SWOOSH!

WE'RE IN A HALLWAY AT the former headquarters of *CSIS*. It's now *The Center for Interdimensional Philosophical Affairs* or, *CIPA*. A self-guided mechanical device is in the process of stenciling lettering onto the opaque window of an office door. Lettering reads,

Director of Epistemics
Bart...

SWOOSH!

The bright flash of an arriving teleporter bursts into view on the other side of the opaque window.

We pull back from the door and continue on. As we go, another door comes into view. It sits adjacent to Bart's. The following is stenciled onto its window,

Director of Aesthetics
Dana Lorre

WE CONTINUE PULLING AWAY, AND on into a world without scarcity.